"We're all working so hard at getting my sister back into her house."

Callie paused, took a deep breath and then said, "I can't take the time to meet with you and your attorney this week. I hope you understand."

"Sure I do. I'll cancel the appointment," Ethan replied, and added in a low voice, "You can just sign the papers and mail them, Cal. No problem."

There would be a problem, though—a huge one. With a couple of stamps and a signature or two, she could vastly increase her chance of losing her little boy, Luke.

"I think we probably do need to sit down with an attorney to make sure everything's in order," Callie said quickly. "Can it wait awhile, though?"

Until she'd had time to escape to Colorado…and then until she moved, leaving no forwarding address.

Dear Reader,

When I was developing the idea for this story, I figured that my reader letter would include a huge thank-you to the many people who helped south-central Kansans after the November 1998 floods. I still want to thank those people, and I also want to apologize to the fine folks of Augusta. Please note that I haven't flooded your town again. I simply rewrote history, moving the 1998 flood to the present time.

As my own family sat in our west Augusta home the night the floodwaters rushed in, we had no idea about the magnitude of the struggle we were beginning. But we began to solve problems immediately. With our cars destroyed by the water, we had to find affordable transportation quickly. Several dear friends and family members helped with that. Next we had to find temporary housing. Again, a family member came through for us. Our list of difficulties was long, but we discovered that no problem was unsolvable. Eventually we recovered fully. (Although my husband is still cleaning tools.)

I think any marriage reaches a point where struggles begin to overtake the good times, but if the couple tackles those issues one by one, they can make it through to a stronger relationship. Is a story about a married couple romantic? I think so. What could be more romantic than a couple sharing a kiss at their fiftieth wedding anniversary? You just know that they must have weathered so many storms. My hero, Ethan, is stouthearted and gregarious—a type of person I've always enjoyed. And Callie is like so many of us. She recognizes truth deep in her heart, but sometimes she listens harder to those deeply ingrained falsehoods.

Enjoy their happy ending. I'd love to hear from you. Contact me through my Web site at www.kaitlynrice.com.

Kaitlyn Rice

The Late Bloomer's Baby

Kaitlyn Rice

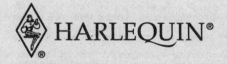

HARLEQUIN®

TORONTO • NEW YORK • LONDON
AMSTERDAM • PARIS • SYDNEY • HAMBURG
STOCKHOLM • ATHENS • TOKYO • MILAN • MADRID
PRAGUE • WARSAW • BUDAPEST • AUCKLAND

ISBN 0-373-75089-7

THE LATE BLOOMER'S BABY

To my editors, Beverley Sotolov, Paula Eykelhof and
Kathleen Scheibling, for your guidance and expert advice.

To Cathy C, for sharing your story about your journey
toward motherhood. Especially for helping with
details about the IVF process.

And to the many people who helped our family recover
from the real Augusta flood in November of 1998:
Mom Marianne, Mom Genny, Jamie and Jane, Billy, Jim,
Mila, Kim and Lud, Connie, the Wilkersons, the Boyds,
Randy's Linda, the Boeing workers, the Red Cross,
the Salvation Army, the National Guard and the folks
at the First Baptist Church, the First Methodist Church,
Robinson School and the Augusta Animal Clinic.

In memory of Randy Qualls and Donna Foulke.

To anyone who helped in any way, thank you.
You helped us make it through.

Books by Kaitlyn Rice

HARLEQUIN AMERICAN ROMANCE
 972—TEN ACRES AND TWINS
1012—THE RENEGADE
1051—TABLE FOR FIVE

Don't miss any of our special offers. Write to us at the
following address for information on our newest releases.

Harlequin Reader Service
U.S.: 3010 Walden Ave., P.O. Box 1325, Buffalo, NY 14269
Canadian: P.O. Box 609, Fort Erie, Ont. L2A 5X3

Prologue

A ringing woke Callie Taylor, and she reached for the alarm switch on her bedside clock. When she realized the sound had come from her phone, she groaned and lifted her head from the pillow to check the time.

Who would be calling at five-twenty in the morning?

It was probably a wrong number. Since she used her machine to screen calls, she'd set it to answer after one ring. She could sleep for a while and check for a message later.

But the timing of the call nagged her until she shoved her covers aside and padded from her bedroom. Pausing at the nursery doorway, she peered inside. Fortunately, the noise hadn't disturbed Luke. Her eleven-month-old son lay flat on his back with his arms and legs flung across the mattress. Callie grinned as she continued toward the phone. Asleep or awake, her dark-haired sweetheart embraced life vigorously.

He was so much like his father.

Callie lost her smile at that thought, but shrugged off her regret. If anyone could revive the ignorant hopes of a newlywed bride, it wasn't Callie. She excelled at science, not men.

After entering her great room, she heard her younger sister finishing a message and grabbed the phone. "Hey, Isabel. What's going on? It's not even six here in Denver."

"Sorry about the early call. I…well, I needed to talk to you."

Her hesitancy alerted Callie to trouble. She sank onto the sofa and tucked her bare legs beneath her nightgown. "What happened, hon?"

"The house flooded, Cal. Pretty bad. I'm calling from a church shelter."

A sense of powerlessness socked Callie in the gut. Her sister lived five hundred and thirty miles away in Augusta, their south-central Kansas hometown. She might as well be across a sea.

"Lord, Izzy! Are you okay?"

"I'm fine. So far, everyone is safe and accounted for."

"Thank God."

"I was home in bed when it happened, though." Isabel's voice vibrated as if she was trembling. "I heard a noise around three-thirty. Something like a crack or a pop. I got up to look around—for some reason the lights worked—and watched the basement fill as if it were a giant bathtub." She laughed nervously. "I think the sound was a window breaking."

Callie sat forward, hugging her knees as she began to shiver, too. "Did you leave then?"

"Well, no. The water was almost to the top of the porch. I couldn't drive out so I called the Augusta police. A National Guard boat picked me up twenty-five minutes later. They took me to a big truck where other evacuees were waiting, and later they brought us all here to the church."

Callie pictured her sister standing in the doorway of their childhood home, awaiting a middle-of-the-night rescue by strangers. She imagined her now, shaking and striving for bravery.

A thought struck then, and Callie pressed a palm against the growing knot in her stomach. Isabel had said that *everyone* was safe. That she was at a *shelter.* Apparently, more than just Isabel's house had flooded.

Callie's youngest sister also lived in Augusta. The Blume home was outside city limits to the south. Josie rented an apartment right in town. "Have you heard from Josie?" she asked.

"She's fine. She said neighborhoods northeast of the middle school weren't affected."

Callie drew in a deep breath.

"The sirens woke her, though. She turned on the news and heard we were flooding. She tried to get to the house but the roads were impassable. She'd just returned when I called a minute ago. She's on her way here to pick me up."

Good. Her sisters were safe. They'd have each other until Callie arrived. "I'll make arrangements and fly into Wichita today," she said. "I can rent a car at the airport so we'll have another vehicle to use, and we'll—"

"Oh, no," Isabel butted in, her voice firm. "I wanted you to know that Josie and I were safe, but you don't need to come. You've got your work to think about, and, well, everything would be too difficult, wouldn't it?"

"Are you kidding? I'll take a leave of absence from BioLabs. My assistants can continue the trials. I need to be with my little sisters."

"But you also have a baby to worry about," Isabel said. "I don't expect you to bring Luke. For the obvious reasons."

Callie frowned through her sister's patient explanation. Yes, her child would complicate this trip, and not simply because he was an infant.

Luke's father lived in Wichita again now—just twenty miles west of Augusta. Ethan didn't know—*couldn't know*—of his son's existence.

"I have no choice but to bring Luke," Callie said, then heard a muffled male voice in the background, followed by Isabel's response. Someone had lured her sister away from their conversation.

Seconds later, she came on the line again. "Sorry. People are waiting for the phone." Isabel lowered her voice. "I did hear you, though. Are you sure you want to take the chance? Josie and I can handle things here, you know."

That was right. Isabel had always been content to piggyback her emotions on the well-being of others, hadn't she? It wasn't that she didn't feel her own feelings, but she derived such joy from her interactions with others. Such energy from their happiness. Even through this trauma, she'd appreciate Josie's spunk. She would be fine. Maybe Callie could stay here in Denver, where she could keep Luke safe.

The man interrupted again. While her sister spoke to him, Callie considered taking the easy out.

No. Despite the risk, she had to go. At twenty-nine, Callie was the oldest of the Blumes. Now that their mother was gone, she felt protective of her sisters. Although Josie and Isabel were each smart and capable, they could surely use an extra brain and pair of hands.

"I'm coming," she insisted when Isabel returned. "I'll call Josie's cell number when I know details about my arrival. We can talk then."

After she hung up, Callie sat on the sofa for a moment, organizing her morning. She'd rush a shower, then pack for two. Later she'd call a travel agency. If she left Luke at the lab's on-site day care for an hour, she could outline a task list for her assistants.

She'd be fine. She probably wouldn't run into Ethan. If she did, she'd control her reaction.

When she caught herself toying with her wedding band and allowing her mind to wander, Callie sighed and rubbed her fingertips across her tired eyes.

She had no choice, really. She was headed home.

Chapter One

Three mornings had passed since heavy rains had caused the Walnut and Whitewater rivers to overflow. The floodwaters had receded now, but hundreds of homes had been abandoned. The muddy devastation at Isabel's house had been tough to see. Turbid water had not only filled the basement, but had risen three feet onto the main floor.

Yesterday, a van load of volunteers had helped her sister cart much of the wreckage to the curb, but the pungent smells and endless mud would be harder to remove. Isabel wouldn't even be allowed to live in the house until the damaged walls and systems had been repaired and inspected.

She'd need all the help she could get. Callie knew she'd been right to come. In spite of the necessity for plans and contingency plans.

In spite of her turmoil.

For the past hour, she'd been in the Hilltop Church gymnasium. After completing financial aid applications for Isabel, she'd joined dozens of others awaiting counsel from relief workers. The molded plastic seats were sticky, the area smelled like a neglected clothes hamper and folks were plainly too weary for small talk.

Callie had alternated between wondering about Luke's welfare down a corridor in the nursery, and imagining Ethan appearing through the gym's open double doors.

If he did, she'd be fine. He wouldn't see her with Luke. She'd only have to deal with the trauma of seeing him again. However, as soon as possible, she intended to get her baby boy and escape to a place less public.

Good thing Ethan was from Wichita. He'd spent time in Augusta with Callie while they were dating, but he didn't know many people here and vice versa. Chances were good that no one would talk to Ethan about her or her baby.

When her number was called, Callie clutched the clipboard to her chest and strode to the opposite end of the gym, where various relief agencies had set up temporary workstations.

"Let's have a look, Miz Blume." The worker met Callie's gaze briefly as he took the paperwork, then he waved her into a chair across the table from him.

Callie wasn't a Blume anymore, of course, but she didn't bother to correct him. He looked vaguely familiar. He must remember her from her youth.

She hadn't really considered herself a married woman for almost two years, anyway. Not since the day Ethan had abandoned their marriage and her life.

The man knit his brow as he read the application, then clicked his pen top once against the table as he turned the page. When he flipped the paper back, his scowl deepened.

Callie leaned forward in her chair, trying to see if she'd neglected to answer some question. When the man turned the page again with a heavy sigh, she reminded herself to be patient. She had no reason to worry. She'd analyzed every response as if it were test data.

The worker tossed the forms on top of his sizable stack, and Callie waited for him to speak. No matter whom he was helping, he should offer some instruction now, as well as a few kind words. But he didn't. He sighed again and sat back in his seat, glaring past her head at the waiting crowd.

When Callie didn't automatically vacate her chair, he repeatedly clicked his pen against the table. "'Bout six weeks," he said, then he clicked two more times before calling the next number.

Callie hadn't been dismissed so rudely in a long time. She realized she was holding her limbs stiff, bracing herself against bitter memories. Of her mother, chasing outsiders from the yard with a pellet gun. Of the whispers she'd heard during her family's rare visits to town. To the folks in Augusta, she would probably always be one of those Blume girls—a little pitiable, a bit mysterious and different enough to be feared.

But this man's behavior, today, didn't matter. Callie had returned to help her family, not to change people's minds. She forced herself to relax, then stood and headed toward the open double doors. She'd locate her son in the nursery and get out of here.

Luke had plopped down in the middle of a round rag rug where several other toddlers were exploring a scattering of toys. While Callie approached, she watched her gregarious son hand a colorful block to a cute blonde who looked about his age, then another to a bigger boy.

Some days, everything Luke did reminded her of Ethan, and she spent a lot of time yearning for those wrecked hopes, and wishing that father and son could know each other.

But the risks would be too great. Just the thought of losing Luke caused Callie's heart to race.

She had control, she reminded herself as she breathed slowly. Her husband had had only one contact with any of the Blumes over the past twenty-two months.

Before she'd come to Denver for Christmas last year, Isabel had run into him at a Wichita department store. Despite her affection for Ethan, she had let him know that the Blume women stuck together. That he should stay out of their lives.

Ethan probably wouldn't come.

Callie was fine.

She picked up her son and cuddled him close, chuckling when he patted her cheeks and said, "Mum-mum."

After thanking the nursery attendants, Callie retrieved her portable stroller from the coat closet, wrangled it open and clipped her son inside. She looped the diaper-bag strap over her shoulder, then wheeled Luke into the hallway.

As she prepared to enter the chill of a mid-April morning, she crouched down to zip Luke's tiny red jacket and lift the hood over his dark brown hair. "Ready to go to Aunt Josie's?" she asked.

In answer, Luke stuck a finger in his grinning mouth.

Callie smiled, happy that at least he'd have two loving aunts in his life. She stood and pushed the stroller toward the parking lot. People were too busy to pay much attention, but she didn't want to be seen often with Luke.

On her way to the rental car, Callie reminded herself that Ethan had chosen the estrangement, not her. Yet if he learned about Luke, she'd risk losing the baby.

Ethan was Luke's biological parent.

Callie wasn't.

Thanks to a miracle of science, Ethan had actually left before she got pregnant. The fertility treatments had failed during the previous twenty-six cycles, so she'd held little hope for that last set of appointments at the clinic. And, after all, her husband had left her six weeks before.

However, Ethan's presence hadn't been necessary, and Callie had needed only to prepare her body for pregnancy and undergo the procedure. She'd imagined how wonderful life would be if her husband came home to such happy news, and she'd tried one last time.

She'd gotten lucky.

A precious life had implanted itself in her womb, and she'd maintained the pregnancy. In the end, it hadn't even mattered that she'd had to use a donor egg. Only that she carried Ethan's child. She'd been overjoyed.

But Ethan had never returned.

Callie hadn't been able to overcome her broken heart to seek him out and tell him. She'd been alone when she decided to keep those last appointments. She'd been alone when she nurtured herself through pregnancy and childbirth. She'd gone on with her life. Precious Luke was hers alone.

Life would be easier if she thought of Ethan as an impartial sperm donor.

By the time she'd loaded Luke into his car seat, his bottom eyelids were turning pink. He'd been a trouper through all this, but the change in routine must bother him. Maybe he'd fall asleep on the way to Josie's place.

After buckling him in, Callie pulled his favorite teddy bear from a diaper-bag pocket. She cranked the gear on its back that would play a tinkling version of Brahms's "Lullaby," then handed the toy to her son before loading the rest.

As she drove away from the church, she wondered how much progress her sister had made with the cleanup. In addition to the house, Isabel had inherited Blumecrafts, their mother's home-based quilt and handmades business. She had no choice but to recover quickly.

Minutes later, Callie parked behind Josie's building and noticed Isabel's used two-door under the carport. Thanks to her auto insurance coverage, she'd replaced her destroyed vehicle yesterday. Unfortunately, her homeowner's policy didn't cover flood damage. Either her sister had dropped by to find out what Callie had learned from the financial aid people, or something had happened.

Callie opened the rental car's back door and released Luke from his child seat. She chuckled when he squealed and bounced in her arms. Even after his too-short nap, he'd awakened easily and happily.

So much like his father.

Callie shuffled Luke onto a hip, grabbed the diaper bag, decided to leave the stroller in the trunk and locked the car before heading toward the building. Seconds later, she walked straight into Josie's apartment through the open hallway door.

She found Isabel in the kitchen scrubbing grime from a sinkful of small craft tools. "Maybe you can leave the front door open at the house," Callie said, "but you shouldn't do that here. Anyone could come in."

Isabel didn't turn around. She had pulled her brown hair off her neck, emphasizing a tired droop to her shoulders. "Sorry," she said. "The kids went out to look at my car a minute ago. They thought it was new, instead of new to me. Guess they forgot about the door."

What kids?

Callie frowned as a tiny girl of above five and an overweight boy maybe twice her age, each redheaded, came running into the hallway from Josie's bedroom. The boy yelled something about the electronic game in his hand, while the girl tried to snatch it. After pausing to check out Callie and Luke, they took their noisy argument down the hallway and back to the bedroom.

"Who are they?" Callie asked, dropping Luke's diaper bag on the kitchen table.

"Roger Junior and Angie."

Callie had spent the past couple of days watching divorced farmer Roger Senior neglect her sister, but she hadn't met his children until now. She frowned as the little girl's shrieks grew louder. "Why are they here?" she asked.

"I'm babysitting." Isabel glanced over her shoulder and smiled, which was amazing under the circumstances. She was temporarily homeless and scrubbing her fingers raw, yet once again her boyfriend was exploiting her giving nature.

And once again, Isabel was allowing it.

Callie put Luke down to crawl around on the floor, then crossed the room and put her hands on her sister's shoulders. As she pulled them into a healthier position, she said, "You'll strain your neck muscles. Don't you have important things to do today?"

Isabel dropped a quilting hoop onto a towel and turned around to lean against the counter. "Yes, but Roger had some barley to check and the kids' school is closed this week," she said. "The kindergarten corridor got half an inch of floodwater."

"Roger should have kept his children home," Callie said. "They are surely old enough to be alone an hour with their dad on the property. Especially the boy."

Isabel closed her eyes, as if trying to block the censure in Callie's expression. "He gets more done with them gone."

"Where's their mom?"

"Working at the discount mart."

As her sister listed excuses for Roger and his ex-wife, Callie lifted her brows. After a minute, she sighed. She had often told her patient sister that Isabel would go berserk if she didn't learn to stand up for herself, but if the devastation of a flood didn't do it, Callie didn't know what would.

Luke crawled toward the kitchen door, clearly lured by the hooting coming from the bedroom. Callie chased after him and scooped him into her arms before he moved out of sight.

"Anyway, it's okay," Isabel said. "Since you're here, I can go to the house. Do you mind watching three kids for a while?"

"Nope." Callie intended to give her sister whatever help she needed. As she transferred Luke from one arm to the other, she realized she hadn't told Isabel about her morning at the church. "I filed the paperwork," she said.

"Did they tell you anything?"

"Just that you'd hear within six weeks," Callie said. "But I did learn that some charities are offering immediate aid in smaller amounts. I'll check that out tomorrow."

"I need money right away," Isabel said, her blue eyes wide. "I'll have to hire an electrician, a plumber and a couple of carpenters. We can't handle the more complicated repairs, and I'm already behind on Blumecrafts' orders."

"I know. This money is meant for toiletries and clothes." Dropping into a chair with Luke in her arms, Callie added, "I also learned that you aren't the only one who got caught without flood insurance, Izzy. I heard a FEMA guy say he figured that less than a hundred Augustans were covered."

"But there are eight thousand people living here!"

Callie nodded, then smiled at her sister. "When I was waiting to turn in the paperwork, I got the strangest feeling. Everyone in the waiting area looked overworked, maybe a little lost. For once, I felt like one of them."

"I guess if there's an upside to this flood, it's that we Blumes are just a part of the crowd," Isabel said. "And of course that we get to spend time together. I miss having you around, Cal."

Their reclusive mother hadn't trusted school officials, and had taught Callie and her sisters at home from kindergarten through high school graduation. For the most part, she had kept them at home, isolated from a world she considered evil. They'd felt like three against the world. Sometimes, they still did.

"I miss you and Josie, too." Callie studied her youngest sister's colorful kitchen. "You'll be okay with money, I think. I'll help with the bigger expenses until your funds come through, and Josie can help you refinish the inside of the house without it costing too much. We're lucky to have an interior designer as a sister."

As Isabel nodded her agreement, a loud scream sounded from the bedroom. Both women winced, and Luke's wiggles grew more vigorous. "I hope Josie doesn't mind having kids in her apartment," Isabel said. "Or us cramping her space."

"She'll get over it."

Roger's children raced into the kitchen, and Roger Junior interrupted the conversation to ask if he and his birdbrained sister could watch television. Then the children continued their squabbling in loud whispers that made Luke giggle.

Had the entire world become bad mannered, or only the

people in Augusta? Callie caught her sister's eye and shook her head. Then she glared at the kids until they quieted.

"Well, Isabel, as you were saying, I'm here now," Callie said, hoping to send a clear message that interruptions would not be tolerated. "You can go on over to the house."

After Isabel had disappeared into Josie's bedroom to get ready, Callie narrowed her gaze at Roger Junior. "One hour of television. Nothing lewd or violent."

She followed them into the living room, where they flopped onto the carpet in front of the TV. When Roger Junior got up to grab a bag of chips from the top of Josie's refrigerator, Callie stopped him. "No snacks in the living room," she said, and ignored his complaints.

She left Luke on the living-room floor and waited for her sister to appear from the bedroom. "Will Roger's kids eat lunch here?" she asked as Isabel carried a box of plastic gloves and some bottled cleaners to the front door.

"Roger should arrive to get them any minute," Isabel said. "If he doesn't, there's peanut butter in the pantry."

After Isabel left, Callie latched a baby gate across the kitchen entrance, shut the bathroom and bedroom doors and tossed a soft ball on the floor for Luke to chase around.

"You kids help me keep the baby safe, would you?" she bellowed over the noise of some cartoon. "If you open this gate, close it behind you. Doors, too."

Roger Junior pressed the mute button on the TV remote control and glanced up. "Sure, ma'am."

Callie noticed the change. With Isabel gone, the boy had become more respectful. Callie would guess that he took his cues from his father.

"Ma'am?"

"Yes?"

"Are you really a doctor?"

Grateful for his belated show of manners, Callie smiled. "Yes. I'm not an M.D., though. I'm a research scientist."

"You look at human brain cells in petri dishes?"

"Sometimes, yes."

The boy stuck his thumb up between them and scrunched his entire face into a smile. "Call me R.J.," he said before he turned up the sound and returned his attention to the cartoon.

Callie chuckled, suspecting she'd just been given a supreme compliment.

"Can I pway wif your baby?" Angie asked.

Callie showed her how to roll the ball to Luke, and kept watching until all three kids were occupied. Then she climbed over the baby gate to search Luke's diaper bag for a bottle.

Someone rang the doorbell. Must be the kids' dad. Callie decided she'd offer to babysit for a while longer so Roger could hightail it to the house to help his girlfriend.

"R.J., answer the door, please," she hollered, as she crossed to the kitchen sink to fill the bottle with water. "I'll be there in a sec."

Callie heard the door open, then an extended silence. She poked her head around the corner just in time to watch a tall, dark-haired man close the door behind himself.

But it wasn't Roger.

It was Ethan.

The only man Callie had ever loved or trusted, and the only man who could hurt her.

Then. Now.

Forever.

Lord. In all the commotion, she'd forgotten her all-important plan. She wasn't supposed to answer doorbells when she and Luke were alone. She should have thought harder about who might be standing on the other side of that door.

Luke sat facing the front door and smiling with the golden-brown eyes and dimpled cheeks that made him the spitting image of his daddy.

Rethinking her plan wasn't an option. Callie barely remembered to keep her legs under her body. She propped a hand against the baby gate and watched as Ethan surveyed the children sprawled around Josie's living room.

Did his eyes linger when they passed over his son, or was that Callie's imagination?

Ethan's gaze sailed across the space to meet hers. "Hello, Callie," he said. As he stepped farther into the room, his eyes darkened to a serious brown.

He'd reacted to seeing her, not the baby, she realized.

Lucky thing. Callie's secret was safe for the moment.

Still, her pulse pounded so furiously in her ears that she had the crazy notion Ethan could hear it, too. Her throat was dry, and her muscles were wobbly.

She needed to sit down.

No, she needed to grab her baby and make a run for it. But Luke was very near his father, which would mean that Callie would have to dash right past Ethan on her way out.

Right past the solid chest that had caught a million of her tears. Right past those muscular arms, and that passionate mouth.

That damn sexy, passionate mouth.

When her stomach flipped, Callie had the panicky thought that her raging feelings didn't stem from fear alone. Ethan was achingly handsome, and she'd missed him.

Desire assaulted her so hard she almost forgot she had

a secret to protect. She wanted nothing more than to cross the room to touch Ethan, just to feel the crackle and comfort of a sensuality she'd never experienced with anyone else.

It had been too long since she'd seen her husband. Paradoxically, it hadn't been nearly long enough.

Chapter Two

Ignoring her body's idiotic fight-or-flight response, Callie stepped over the baby gate to enter Josie's living room. "Hello," she said coolly, as if Ethan was an acquaintance she hadn't seen in a while. She sat on the sofa, propped the bottle against the cushion next to her and crossed her legs, as if she had nowhere to go and nothing to lose.

Ethan shook his head. "Is Josie dating a man with kids, or are you running a child care center?"

The presence of Roger's kids was fortunate. Callie wouldn't have to strain her temporarily useless brain cells. Obviously, Ethan had assumed that Luke belonged with the other two children.

She studied the two redheaded kids, then Luke. The baby's hair was almost black. Except for the curls at his neck that Callie adored too much to snip off just yet, it was thick and straight—just like Ethan's.

Her lively boy shrieked and threw the ball straight at Angie's face, bonking the little girl on the nose. A mischievous little brother would do such a thing, wouldn't he? Callie could use the situation to her advantage.

"Isabel's got the boyfriend with kids, not Josie," she

mumbled, hoping the children wouldn't notice her error of omission. "Why are you here?"

He didn't answer immediately. He stared at the kids, then caught the ball as it rocketed toward the baby's face. He bounced it on his palm a couple of times, then tossed it to Callie.

"No face shots," she said as she returned the ball to Angie. "The little guy doesn't have good motor control yet. He didn't mean to hit you."

Callie looked at Ethan and wished she had the ball back. She wanted to bonk his nose and shock that warm expression from his eyes.

"I came to check on Isabel, but no one was home when I went by her house a few minutes ago," Ethan said.

"She just left to head out there. You must have passed her on the road."

"I'll give her a few minutes and try again." He claimed the chair by the door, which happened to be the one nearest his son—who threw back his head and cackled exactly the way Ethan did when he was tickled.

Someone was going to notice the resemblance.

Callie swooped across the room and grabbed Luke, then returned to sit on the sofa and offer him the bottle of water.

Everyone in the room stared at her.

"It's time for his nap," she announced, ignoring her baby's struggle to escape her arms.

Of course, Ethan would check on her sister. In her heart of hearts, Callie had expected him to, hadn't she? As many times as she'd told herself not to worry, that he might not come, she wasn't surprised. Ethan didn't have ties to Augusta anymore, but he'd always had a compulsion to rescue anyone in distress. That was what had attracted him to police work.

To her, as well. She was sure of it now.

The strength of her reaction to him had startled her, though, as had her impulse to smile and ask if he found their son amazing.

God. She could never do that. Ethan had made his choice. He'd returned to Kansas without her. In doing so, he'd forced her to abandon one dream and focus on another.

As Luke's fussy whimper escalated to a lusty bawl, she stood and carried him toward the kitchen.

Ethan spoke over the noise. "I've been listening to flood reports all week. I was off duty the night the water broke through the levee, but my patrol buddies made a few passes and told me about it."

It sounded as if he was following her. Callie stepped over the baby gate and turned around.

He was standing just on the other side. The flimsy plastic slats separating her husband from his fussing child couldn't possibly be tall or thick enough. Callie bounced Luke, trying to soothe him and think at the same time.

She didn't want Ethan's attention on the baby, so she put Luke down and hoped he'd crawl in the other direction.

The ornery little guy sat peering up at his daddy, then hiccuped a few times as his cries subsided.

Ethan chuckled. "I guess the little tyke isn't sleepy after all," he said, and lowered his voice. "Don't worry. You'll get the hang of babysitting. It just takes hands-on experience."

Callie ignored the comment. "You're still in west Wichita, then?"

"I would have told you if I'd moved." He inched forward, until they were separated by only the slats and about a foot of space. But at least he focused on *her* instead of Luke. "I needed time to put our problems into perspective, but I wouldn't lose track of you."

She wondered if that were true, but she couldn't pursue the subject with Luke at her feet and Roger's big-eared, big-mouthed children nearby.

Ethan's ignorance about Luke was crucial.

It would save her son the heartache of growing up with warring parents or living a divided life.

It would save her from having to battle her husband on any front.

And it would save them all from Ethan's unfortunate tendency to do the heroic thing at any cost.

During their courtship, she and Ethan had spent a lot of time discussing her childhood. Callie's father had left when her mother was pregnant with Josie. Despite a fierce independence, Ella Blume had struggled to raise three daughters alone. She'd always insisted that the girls' father was worthless, and that she'd never known an honorable man.

Ethan had wanted to prove Ella wrong, and Callie and Ethan had each wanted to prove they could make their marriage work.

Maybe her mother had been right about some things. Maybe men weren't built for forever. Maybe they did mistake lust for love.

Maybe Ethan had felt only chemistry, a challenge to prove himself and sympathy for a shy young woman who'd had to be taught just about everything.

Callie didn't want to be his project anymore. She certainly didn't want to be the woman he returned to because of a child. She'd loved him deeply. She'd probably always love him—from a distance.

At this moment, Callie wanted to convince Ethan to abandon his thoughts of seeing Isabel, and leave. But how?

She stalled for time by checking Luke's diaper, and when she glanced up she almost groaned at the gleam in Ethan's eye. He was watching her in *that* way. She had to do something, fast.

She'd pick a fight, but keep it low-key. She didn't want to upset Luke again or draw the older kids' attention away from the television—which, she realized in that instant, was silent.

Callie glanced toward the living room. Roger's kids were standing just beyond the sofa, gawking at her and Ethan. Had the hushed adult conversation caught their attention, or were the children expecting a fight? Whichever it was, apparently she and Ethan were more interesting than the latest hit Japanese cartoon.

Smiling at Angie, Callie said, "Josie has Popsicle treats. Want one?" Without waiting for an answer, she opened the freezer and pulled out two red ones—she had neither the energy nor the wits to referee a brawl right now—then she hurdled the gate and strode past Ethan to hand them to the kids. "Eat in here," she commanded. "And watch anything you want on TV."

The markedly confused kids plunked down in their previous places, clicked the television on again and peeled the paper from their treats.

Callie reclaimed her spot on the kitchen side of the gate. "Go away, Ethan. We have too much bad history. Your being here would…" Her voice trailed off when she noted her husband's scowl.

He stepped over the gate, rushed past Callie and caught the diaper bag just before Luke pulled it onto his head. "You have to watch babies this age," Ethan said as he set the bag in the middle of the table. "Some of my friends have them, and they can get into a lot of trouble."

Another calamity averted, by quick-moving Ethan. Callie wasn't usually so slow, except she was distracted. By Ethan, darn him. After crossing the kitchen, Callie stuck her hand in the diaper bag. She located Luke's favorite plastic blocks and tossed them onto the kitchen floor.

Luke ignored them, choosing instead to grasp the knees of Ethan's jeans to pull himself up. The little devil stood on sturdy legs, opened his mouth, looked at Callie and said, "Mum-mum."

Not Mama exactly, but almost.

Callie opened the freezer door and grabbed another red Popsicle. She unwrapped it and handed it to Luke, who plopped his well-padded bottom onto the floor to examine this new kind of food.

As her little boy began to create a colossal mess on his face, hands and clothes, Callie returned her attention to Ethan. "As I was saying, we can't be around each other."

"I think we'd do all right."

Callie shook her head. "The flood put my sister's life in turmoil. Our bickering would make things worse. Just go."

"I have no intention of fighting with you, Callie."

"Believe me, we'd fight." Callie caught a motion out of the corner of her eye and looked down.

Luke was banging his goopy snack against Ethan's shoe.

Ethan looked, too, but he didn't react. "Are you still that upset with me?" he asked, and offered Callie one charming dimple.

She sighed. Her feelings for Ethan were overwhelming, especially with him just inches away, gazing at her through eyes that warmed her faster than any form of external heat.

But anger was still somewhere in the mix.

She nodded.

Ethan eased his foot away from Luke. "Will you be in Kansas for a while or do you have to get back to your job?"

"I took a leave of absence."

"You did?"

"Josie and I are all the family Isabel has, Ethan. I'm not so detached that I'd stay in Denver while she's going through something like this."

He nodded. "All right. Then I'll concede for now," he said. "I'll try Isabel's house again. I want to at least offer her my best wishes."

Callie hesitated. If Ethan went to the house alone, Isabel would refuse to talk to him. She'd follow the plan.

But if Ethan mentioned that he'd been inside Josie's apartment—that he'd spoken to Callie or watched the children playing—Isabel might not know how to react.

Callie stood up straighter, as if to add oomph to her words by speaking them from a higher plane. "She's probably at the house by now, but she's working hard. Let's not disturb her."

Ethan pulled paper towels from Josie's countertop holder and wiped red slush from his shoe. "If she's busy I'll stay only a minute."

Callie extended her open palm. After Ethan had deposited the towel there, she held his gaze and tried to look stern. "You can't go to the house."

"Sure I can."

"Ethaa-nn!"

"Callie!"

She broke the stare and walked toward the sink, intending to toss the towel into Josie's wastebasket. On the way, she stepped in one of Luke's slush puddles, slid on one foot and almost landed on her bottom. She gripped the counter and turned to glower at Ethan, whose expression held a glint of laughter.

She could slap him silly.

Or kiss him.

Lord. How could she even think that? She should have learned her lesson when Ethan had left her.

She *had* learned her lesson.

Apparently, recognizing the wrongness of something didn't stop her from wanting it. But she could resist. Ella Blume had raised strong daughters. And smart ones. Callie could handle this.

Wiping her sneaker with the same paper towel Ethan had used, she scrambled to think of some indisputable reason for him to return to Wichita without seeing her sister.

He spoke first. "Look at the bright side. This way, you won't have to deal with me a minute longer. But you and I should talk before you head back to Colorado."

She tossed the towel on the counter and eyed him. "About what?"

"The marriage," he said, his face impassive. "We are still married."

Yes, they were. If Callie didn't have an irresistibly cute, diaper-clad reason for shying away from legal proceedings, she would have divorced Ethan a long time ago. But she'd never wanted to draw his attention to her life. She'd done some checking soon after Luke's birth, and had learned that a discussion of children showed up on most divorce documents. A couple either had minor children or didn't, and filed papers accordingly.

Even if she'd lied, stating that she and Ethan had no children, she'd feared that Ethan would show up in Denver for one last talk and get the surprise of his life. Now Callie resisted an urge to check on Luke, who had crawled beyond the table and chairs where she couldn't see him.

"I'm surprised you didn't file for divorce," Ethan said.

Callie shrugged. She'd had nightmares about this day. She'd blocked reality, hoping that Ethan would follow in her father's footsteps and disappear, still legally married but uninterested in active participation. While that might have been a pipe dream, it had worked for her mother. It had worked for Callie for almost two years.

Why not forever?

Ethan jangled his keys in his pocket and stepped over the baby gate. Callie couldn't let him go to the house alone. With Isabel's phone out of commission, she couldn't even call to warn her sister about the slight change in plans.

"I'll go with you," Callie said, searching the kitchen floor for Luke.

"Wouldn't that defeat your goal?" Ethan said. "I thought you wanted me out of your way."

She wanted him to leave without discussing a divorce, and if she spent much time in his company she feared the subject would come up.

She ignored his comment. "Give me a minute to change the baby," she said. Then she grabbed sticky Luke from beside the microwave stand and the diaper bag from the table, and vaulted past Ethan. She turned off the television on her way to the bathroom.

"Kids, finish the Popsicle treats. We're going to Isabel's."

"Dad says her place isn't safe," R.J. said as he scrambled to his feet.

Callie stepped into the bathroom and opened both sink

taps. "You'll be fine," she hollered as she soaked a wash-rag and cleaned Luke's face. "The floodwater has been pumped out. Just avoid anything that looks dangerous."

"Can your baby go?" Angie called out. "Daddy says the water was com*bob*-ulated!"

"That's contaminated, birdbrain," R.J. said.

But it was Angie's little-girl sweet voice that reverberated in Callie's mind.

Your baby, she'd said.

Not *the* baby.

Callie cringed, then carried Luke into the hallway to gauge Ethan's reaction. He was standing by the front door, checking his wallet. He didn't appear to have heard, thank heaven.

"Don't worry about the baby," Callie said to Angie. "And don't worry about your safety. I'll protect all of you."

Roger's kids gave her funny looks, but she ignored them and returned to the bathroom to finish getting Luke ready. Their opinions about her sanity meant very little.

Ethan's continued cluelessness was paramount.

As HE DROVE TOWARD the old Blume house, Ethan felt a hollowness in his gut. Officials were still speculating about why the levee had failed. Even if engineers determined a cause, affected folks would probably always fear heavy rains. Or they'd move to higher ground.

The neighborhood of small row houses at the southernmost tip of Augusta had been hit hard. Tall piles of ruined furniture lined the curbs and smaller pieces of garbage had drifted everywhere. Limbs and soggy papers dotted driveways and lawns, old tires rested on budding bushes, and some kid's plastic play gym adorned the middle of an elaborate garden. The upturned slide matched the color of the jonquils blooming at the garden's edge.

Those bright little beacons of hope couldn't be cheerful enough. A lot of people had a lot of work to do. Some would have to start over entirely.

It was just as bizarre to travel the few miles out of town with Callie trailing him like a bloodhound on the scent of a fugitive. His normally cautious wife had already run one red light in her effort to keep up with him, and her eyes were glued to his car's bumper.

She was acting very strange.

Maybe she was as affected as he was by the reunion. Sweet mercy, she was beautiful. Her long blond hair had always been pretty, but today it looked thicker. Her boyishly thin body had filled out, too. He'd always admired her legs, but the added curves made her almost too powerfully feminine.

He'd always suspected that she'd be a late bloomer.

He wondered if she had someone to confide in these days—someone other than her sisters, who held many of the same distorted beliefs that she did.

Callie was brilliant in every way but socially. She might help find a cure for cancer someday, but she couldn't see that her mother had been wrong to bundle all men together and toss them out like last week's newspaper.

Ethan had rescued Callie, once. He'd pulled her away from her mother's erroneous teachings and into life. He'd relished his protective role until the stresses of energy-zapping careers, Ella's death and carefully timed love-making had torn them apart.

During that last year, they'd hardly been friends.

The separation had probably convinced Callie that her mother had been right all along, but Ethan couldn't worry about that any longer. His days of proving his devotion to Callie were finished.

He'd come to Augusta to check on Isabel, just as he'd said, but he'd known all along that he intended to speak to Callie if he saw her. He'd had divorce papers ready for over three months, ever since his first date with his chief's niece last New Year's Eve.

Dating LeeAnn felt wrong since he wasn't legally free, but he'd hated the idea of sending the papers to Callie by courier. He'd made plans to fly to Denver several times, but something had always come up. On one of his free weekends, LeeAnn had invited him to her mother's birthday celebration. Another time he'd been called in off-duty to help locate a four-year-old girl who had vanished from her grandmother's backyard. Often the end of his shift didn't correspond with the end of his call-out, and he used his off hours to recuperate.

Maybe he'd avoided the task for other reasons. After loving a woman like Callie, dating again was difficult. But it was time to move on and he knew it.

Ethan would talk to Callie long enough to assure himself of her well-being, then he'd tell her about the papers and make arrangements for the two of them to meet with his lawyer. He'd pay for the whole shebang, and if she asked for anything he'd be generous. Callie had nothing to lose, and LeeAnn would be pleased.

He glanced in the rearview mirror, ensuring that Callie was still behind him as he drove up to the house.

Set back from the road about thirty yards, the old Blume homestead was surrounded by lush trees and bushes. Ella had cherished her privacy. Today, the house also sported a lonely pile of discards near the ditch. A floral sofa rested atop a mattress, which was piled on top of quite a few other ruined items. Ethan could imagine the destruction inside. Isabel must be very shaken.

After unfastening his seat belt, Ethan pulled his checkbook from the glove box. He could at least offer Callie's sister some financial help. Since he wouldn't need to fly to Denver to talk to Callie about the divorce, he could put that money to better use.

Two car doors slammed, then Ethan watched the two older children emerge from Callie's car and race toward the house. Callie followed, lugging the youngest boy and the diaper bag.

Ethan opened the door, stepped out and slipped the checkbook into a hip pocket. It hurt to see how easily Callie balanced the smallest child on her hip. She'd wanted children—she'd *ached* for them. Babysitting must be tough for her.

Callie didn't glance backward at the sound of his car door slamming, and she appeared to be in an awful hurry. She opened the storm door and the inside door for the kids, followed them inside and closed the doors behind her.

Ethan stopped in the drive. Boorish behavior was Callie's biggest pet peeve. Perhaps she'd forgotten he was right behind her and planning to come inside.

Or maybe she didn't want to see him.

He stepped onto the porch and knocked on the storm door. Callie couldn't have gone far. If she didn't answer, he was prepared to let himself in. Hell, he'd bust the door down if necessary. And he wouldn't leave until he learned why his normally cool wife was acting crazy. In the past, she'd lost her composure only when they were arguing.

Or when they were in bed.

The memory sent a rush of want through his body, and left him standing on Isabel's porch feeling half-turned-on.

Sweet mercy. He couldn't think about Callie that way.

He opened the storm door and scanned the interior door for weak places to bust through. Before he could knock, however, Isabel answered. Her hair had fallen from a bun and she wore a stained sweatshirt.

After they'd greeted each other, she stood smiling at him, but she didn't come out and she kept her body wedged in the narrow crack.

He wasn't surprised. Apparently, Callie's sisters thought she needed their protection. "You're not going to ask me in, are you?"

"Uh, no."

He pulled out his checkbook. "I'm going to help someone in this town, even if it's just to donate money. I'd prefer it if that someone was you."

"Oh." Isabel blinked. "You don't have to give me money, Ethan. I'll be okay."

"It's your choice," he said. "I'll donate three hundred bucks to you personally, or I'll let the Salvation Army distribute it however they see fit."

"Oh. Well, great. I'm sure they can use the help. Thanks." Isabel smiled.

"I'd rather help someone I know," he said. "And if you take my money, I'll get some of my work buddies to help with a larger donation for charity."

Isabel still seemed unconvinced, so he raised his eyebrows and pointed his thumb over his shoulder. "A few hundred dollars might replace that sofa out there."

She sighed heavily. "All right."

"I need a pen." Ethan had a pen, but he hoped this latest ploy would get him past the door.

"Just a minute." When Isabel shut the door in his face, Ethan realized she intended to find a pen and bring it out.

He pushed the door open and stepped inside. When he heard murmurs overhead, he realized that Callie and the kids must be hiding in Isabel's attic storeroom.

That was fine. Strange, but fine. They wouldn't stay up there long. Callie wouldn't want the children to be frightened in the dark, stuffy space.

As he waited for Isabel, Ethan wandered into the living room. It was devoid of furniture, the carpeting had been stripped and the walls showed a dingy line of discoloration from the water. The wet wallboard would need to be replaced. The insulation, too.

When Isabel returned, she acted surprised to discover him inside. "Oh! Ethan, you're in here," she said in a loud voice that bounced off the bare walls.

He'd been announced, and he didn't care. He frowned at Isabel and waved a hand at the room's mess. "I'm sorry about all this, Izzy."

"It's hard to look at, isn't it? Anything below three feet was ruined by the water, including every *single* thing in the basement. Mom's old textbooks, the boxes of Christmas things." She smiled sadly. "Remember that old cedar chest?"

Yes, he did. Ella had refused to tell Callie and her sisters about the old piece, so they believed it had belonged to their father. "Sure I do," he said.

Isabel shrugged. "It came unglued. The pieces floated everywhere."

Ethan took her hand briefly, offering a consoling squeeze. "Save the pieces," he said. "It could probably be repaired."

She offered him the pen. "Maybe."

As he wrote, he asked, "What are you working on now?"

Isabel sighed. "We're ready to tear out the wallboard and hire a crew to replace it."

At least she was on the right track. "You have people helping you, then?"

"I have plenty of help."

Isabel shot a glance at the ceiling, and Ethan knew Callie was behind her odd behavior. The Blume sisters stuck together no matter what. If he wanted to talk to Callie, he was going to have to entice her from the attic. Isabel wasn't likely to help.

Ethan ripped out the check and handed it to Callie's sister. "Excuse me, Izzy," he said, moving into the hallway.

"Callie, come down," he shouted toward the ceiling. "I know you're in the attic and I'm not leaving until we talk."

Silence. He returned his attention to the blushing Isabel, then crossed the hall to stare up the narrow stairway. "Callie, you're being ridiculous."

Silence. He rested a foot on the bottom step. "I can climb the confounded stairs, Cal."

He heard the hiss of whispering voices, then the girl and boy came down, followed by Callie with the baby. She stopped at the bottom of the steps, ignoring Ethan and bouncing the little boy in her arms as if she was soothing him.

But the baby was already chortling. While Callie scowled.

Hoping to distract her, he gave the little boy a huge smile that prompted one in response. "Cute kid," he said.

Callie's eyes widened, then she glanced at the baby's face and nodded.

Ethan sighed. He couldn't talk to Callie if they spent the day admiring some baby.

"May I?" When he reached out to take the little boy, Callie held on tight.

"Aw, come on," Ethan said, smiling at Isabel. "Would your boyfriend mind if I held the little tyke for a minute?"

"I doubt it." Isabel shot a worried glance at Callie. "It's okay," she said, lifting her brows. "Ethan can hold the baby."

Gray eyes turbulent, Callie handed the kid across.

Ethan talked softly to the baby as he crossed the room with Callie on his heels. He handed the little boy to Isabel, then whipped around and grabbed Callie's wrist. "Let's go somewhere to talk."

She yanked her arm free, then turned around and walked out the front door.

After Ethan had followed his furious, sputtering wife out to the porch, he realized that her thin cotton T-shirt would do little to protect her from the chill.

She'd always been absentminded about dressing for the weather. He'd always enjoyed taking care of her. "Don't you have a jacket?" he asked.

"No." She crossed her arms in front of her. "Let's make this quick. I'm freezing."

He was tempted to offer her his shirt, even if that meant going bare-chested. Undressing in front of her might be a problem, though. If she looked at him in a certain way, he might wonder what she was thinking. Hell, he might hope she was thinking about sex. Seeing her in his shirt might not help, either. She'd worn his shirts after sex when they were together. Sometimes during sex.

He had to keep his mind on his goal—which was to tell her about the divorce.

He couldn't do that yet.

He'd thought he could greet Callie and her sisters as if they were no more than old friends, but reality had reminded him of some complicated feelings—protectiveness, desire, affection.

Rather than callously dropping his news, he wanted to let her get used to seeing him again. Apparently, he could use a little adjustment time himself.

He would tell her, though. Very soon.

Right now, he wanted to find out why she'd insisted on coming here to Isabel's house with him when she was so set on avoiding him. "What's going on, Callie?" he asked.

"What do you mean?"

"You don't want me here at all, do you?"

"No."

"Why not?"

She glared at him. "We shouldn't be around each other at all. Not even to talk privately."

"We're still married, Cal. Why not talk?"

"We have a certificate. We're not exactly married," she said. "You walked out on me, remember?"

Okay, that was true. But they were still married. Their strange situation had entered his thoughts at odd times over the past two years, causing near panic. He wasn't the type to leave things undone.

He didn't want to have this conversation on Isabel's front porch, but he could at least start them talking. "I walked out on a failing relationship."

"There you go."

Callie didn't meet his eyes. Ethan stepped nearer and realized she was watching someone park a battered pickup behind the little white Mazda she was driving.

A redheaded man got out and walked up the drive. At first, Ethan had the blinding thought that the slightly plump man was Callie's boyfriend, and the cause of her irrational behavior.

But then the guy said, "Hi, Callie. No one was home at Josie's apartment. Did Isabel bring my kids here?"

"They're in the house," Callie said.

Aha! The redhead was Isabel's boyfriend. Ethan wondered at his sense of relief. He still cared about Callie and always would, but he didn't expect her to live the life of a hermit.

He didn't intend to do that. He had LeeAnn, who had made her readiness for romance quite apparent. His marriage had failed. He should move on, and be happy for Callie.

"Wait there for one minute until I'm finished here, and I'll go get the kids," Callie hollered at the other man. Then she shot a glance at Ethan and added, "*All* of them."

Man, she'd sounded bossy. Isabel's friend stopped immediately and stood perusing the pile of junk at the end of the drive.

Callie returned her attention to Ethan, her eyes huge. "Okay, you win," she said, speaking quickly. "I'll meet you somewhere later and we can talk."

"I could come in and help."

"No. You have to go now."

For whatever reason, she was rushing him off. Ethan liked the idea of meeting her later, though. He could use the time to think about how to approach the subject of divorce. That shouldn't be hard after a two-year separation, but it was. Apparently, on both sides.

"Tonight at, say, ten o'clock, I'll meet you at Mary's Bar," she said. "You know the place, out off Ohio Street?"

How could he forget it? Before they were married, he and Callie had spent hours making out in the bar's back parking lot. "All right. Mary's at ten."

Callie paused and frowned as if she intended to say more, but then she just tugged on his sleeve. "Come on."

"What are we doing?"

She started down the drive. "Walking to your car."

He laughed. Did she expect *her* boyfriend to show up? Maybe she didn't want to explain Ethan's presence to her new love interest. Come to think of it, maybe the guy didn't know she'd been married.

As much as the thought bothered him, Ethan knew he was probably right. A jealous boyfriend would explain her bizarre behavior. "All right, but you'd better show up," he said as he opened his car door and sank inside. "I know where to find you if you don't."

"I'll be there."

Ethan was much happier to hear those words than he should have been.

Chapter Three

Callie stepped inside the door of Mary's and allowed her senses to adjust. The sharp smell of cigarette smoke made her want to pinch her nose, and the crowded darkness invited trouble. The bar was small and shabby, but it fulfilled a purpose. Local citizens kept the business going because they preferred to drink and mingle without having to drive the extra few miles to a more upscale place.

Since she valued logic over social approval, Callie didn't mind admitting that she preferred clean smells and daylight. She'd never frequented Mary's or any other bar, but she'd wanted a good place to talk to Ethan tonight.

The crowd added safety, yet unless something happened, folks would be uninterested in her and Ethan's conversation. Besides, she'd wanted to meet Ethan late, so she could leave Luke at Josie's apartment without burdening her overworked sisters with his care. He'd been asleep for an hour already, and he'd likely sleep through until morning.

Ethan was here, somewhere. She'd seen his car in the lot. She scanned the space and located him sitting at a table just yards in front of her with his back to the door. Surrounded by four pretty women, he was entertaining them with an anecdote that must be enthralling.

The ladies were all pitched forward in their seats, eyes wide, heads nodding and lips pursed. Suddenly, all four women opened those pouty lips to gasp.

Callie swallowed a lump of jealousy. Ethan had always liked people. All people, not just women. He was probably passing the time, expecting her to be late, as usual. In any case, his behavior was none of her business.

Heavens, he looked good. The sight of his broad shoulders and muscled arms made her wish for things she shouldn't. Ethan had made her feel sexy and soft, instead of just smart. No couple could have had a more romantic beginning. None. Just like the ladies at his table now, she'd brightened in his company.

She'd be tempted to repeat every trial of their marriage, just to relive one of those early days.

If that were possible, however, she'd be wishing Luke right out of her life.

She couldn't do that. Luke *was* her life.

Her deep, crazy wishes hardly mattered, anyway. Ethan had made it clear that he was finished with her. He'd tired of her, just as her mother had predicted.

An outbreak of wild female giggles nearly brought tears to Callie's eyes. She knew her envy didn't make sense. She wasn't supposed to care. She was supposed to be over him, vanishing into her separate life while he vanished into his.

Unfortunately, when it came to Ethan, Callie's emotions often overtook her rational thoughts.

She'd have to be very careful.

She approached the table, stopping at Ethan's side. "I'm here," she said.

Ethan said goodbye to the ladies, then grabbed his bottle of beer and stood. "I couldn't find an empty table a few minutes ago, but we can hunt for one together."

They surveyed the area. Most of the crowd had gathered around the pool tables or the bar. All five tables in the larger room were occupied, but Ethan put a hand at Callie's waist to guide her in that direction.

A single guy sat alone at a table, ogling a petite blonde waiting to order at the bar. Ethan approached, offering the guy a nod in greeting. "Pretty girl," he said. "Interested?"

"Sure as taxes," the man said.

Ethan handed him a bill. "I saw her eyeing you earlier. She's receptive. Go offer to buy her a drink."

"Wow. Thanks, man."

"We'll be taking your table, though."

"No problem."

Callie smiled as they sat down. Ethan was in a friendly mood. Maybe they could talk without getting into an argument. She'd always felt so out of control during their clashes, and she feared that she'd say something she'd forever regret.

Could she convince Ethan that he should simply vanish again, without discussing a divorce?

"You want something to drink?" he asked. "I'm sure they have something nonalcoholic."

She eyed his bottle of beer. She'd never been much of a drinker, but at the moment she wanted something to steady her nerves. "I'd drink one of those."

"Really?"

She nodded.

He raised his eyebrows, then got up and went to the bar. Soon, he returned with two open beers—a fresh one for himself and one for her.

She tipped the bottle to her mouth, wrinkling her nose at the first taste, then took a longer drink. The beer's cold bitterness soothed her dry throat. After another drink, she set the bottle on the table and gazed at him. "It's been nice to see you, Ethan. But after we talk tonight, you should go home and forget about me and my sisters."

He scowled, but he didn't say anything.

"Our relationship is over," Callie added. "I can't think of a single reason for us to spend time together."

"You're serious."

"Absolutely."

"You must have a jealous boyfriend."

Callie stared at him. She hadn't thought of lying about an involvement, but his presumption could be lucky. "Well, I have gone on with my life," she said.

"Then I guess this is a good time to talk," he said. "I've also been dating. The woman's name is LeeAnn Chambers, and she works as a secretary and moonlights as a fiddle player for the River's Bend music group. You heard of them?"

Oh, Lord. He had a girlfriend? Callie didn't want to hear a name, and she most certainly didn't want details. "No, I haven't," she said. She picked up her drink, realized her fingers were shaking and gripped the bottle more firmly. After another long swig, she glared at Ethan as he continued to talk about LeeAnn.

Plunking the drink on the table, Callie looped her hair behind her ears and fixed a stare past his head. Maybe an act of disinterest would make him stop rattling on about this woman.

He did stop.

And he grabbed Callie's left hand. "You're still wearing your wedding ring?" he asked, his expression incredulous.

Damn. She'd forgotten about the ring.

She wore it mostly for convenience. Whenever she took

Luke out in public, people approached her to comment on her baby's dimpled grin or thick hair or bright eyes. She wanted those folks to picture him with a perfect home life, with parents devoted to each other and to him.

The way she'd imagined her life with Ethan.

But part of her reason, too, was that she hadn't found the heart to remove it. The impossibility of a reconciliation didn't keep her from clinging to that old dream, as if it were a long-comatose loved one on life support.

She couldn't tell Ethan any of this.

"I don't think about it," she said, shrugging. "But I've always thought it was pretty."

"Your boyfriend doesn't mind?"

Callie held Ethan's gaze for an endless time. When the floor didn't swallow her up, chair, beer and all, she decided she'd have to keep talking to him.

She couldn't think of a single thing to say.

Ethan tipped up his beer, finishing it, then said, "You don't have a boyfriend at all, do you?"

She shrugged.

"You're trying to evade men's interest," he said. "You're using the ring as protection."

He wasn't too far off target, and his words hurt because he knew her so well.

He knew her so well, yet he'd left her.

"It's none of your business, is it?" she said. "It's my ring. Go away and let me live my life."

Callie got up and wound her way through the crowd. As soon as she'd left the bar, she broke into a jog. She'd almost made it to the car when he caught her elbow.

"Let go of me, Ethan."

He did, and she turned around. She hoped he'd attribute her flush to anger rather than humiliation. Women who were over their exes didn't wear the man's ring, did they? Her mother hadn't worn her father's. Here Callie was, the woman Ethan had left, wearing his wedding ring two years later. He'd suggested that she wore it to hide from other men, but he might also wonder if she was pining away for him. She could hardly explain that she wore it for their baby's sake, damn it.

"I just want to know why," he said. His attention traveled from her eyes to her mouth to her neck.

Her blush flowed downward, until she was hot everywhere.

"Why, Callie?"

Sweet heaven, she couldn't think when he looked at her that way.

She didn't want to think.

She had so much to lose if she got involved with him again. Why not kiss him one last time—really kiss him—while she had the chance?

She grabbed his T-shirt and tugged him nearer.

Before his chiseled lips touched hers, he parted them. He tasted sexy, like cold beer and hot, wild seduction. As his warm breath flowed into Callie's mouth, the reminder of their lusty early days hit her, hard.

Her knees wobbled. Her breasts ached. Her womb opened.

She wanted nothing more than for Ethan to touch her, long and lovingly, everywhere she ached.

That could never happen again.

Still, she didn't move away from him. The unaccustomed alcohol in her system had probably made her reckless. It also didn't help that they were standing in the same parking lot where she'd first learned how to love a boy in every way. His hands settled low on her hips, and she leaned into him. She'd always loved it when he pulled her to him and flaunted his body's need for her.

But this time, he propelled her backward.

His expression showed confusion, but Callie could still feel his passion down to her bones. She could still see it in the flash of his eyes and in his quick, deep breaths.

Man, she'd missed that look.

In the end, when they were battling over everything from laundry duties to where they should live, she'd stopped seeing any signs he wanted her. She'd thought his desire was gone forever.

It *needed* to be gone forever.

And Callie needed to think her way through this situation. Of course, their reunion reminded her of the good things. Ethan had made Callie feel beautiful, once.

He'd made her feel alive.

As much as she'd missed him—as much as it tore her heart out to let this man go again, even for a moment— she couldn't forget the reason for the separation.

Leaving had been his choice. A thousand wishes hadn't brought him home, and now Callie had a baby she couldn't fathom losing.

A baby whose identity she couldn't risk revealing.

Fisting her hands to keep them from trembling, Callie perched them against her hips and said, "What would your fiddle player think if she realized we still have that level of heat between us?"

He scowled.

"That's why, Ethan. That's why you have to go away and leave me alone."

"I wanted to talk to you about unfinished business tonight, Callie. About our marriage. I didn't intend to start anything else." He shook his head. "Maybe we need a chaperone."

She glanced around. They were alone out here, but someone might come or go at any time. "We aren't going to discuss anything in Mary's parking lot."

"I didn't plan to have the discussion out here."

"You followed me out."

His jaw tensed. "You get your way, don't you, Cal?"

She didn't think so. She might have maneuvered her way out of a conversation tonight—she hoped so—but she for damn sure hadn't gotten her way.

She felt an almost frantic desire to keep Ethan near, but she couldn't. Not if she wished to raise Luke in the way every child deserved—in one home, by the person who had nurtured him from his first second of life.

"Cal?"

She shrugged, pretending this wasn't hell for her, too. "Guess so."

He sighed. "I'm suddenly in no mood to talk tonight, but get it in your head that we will have this conversation very soon. Deal?"

She lifted her chin and didn't answer.

Ethan looked at her for another few seconds. Then he finally strode across the parking lot. He got in his car, started it and drove away. Callie watched until he turned right onto the highway and traveled out of sight.

She stood in the same spot for a few minutes afterward, imagining that sweet, lost desire and something else she missed just as much: feeling safe enough to be honest with Ethan.

But losing him had taken a lot out of her. Sharing her days with their sweet baby kept her whole and peaceful. If she lost her little boy, she might become bitter.

She might become her mother.

For the life of her, she couldn't take that risk.

A WEEK LATER, Ethan sipped his water and watched the breakfast crowd at Wichita's Beacon Restaurant. After it had become apparent that his odd working hours and Lee-Ann's weekend concert bookings weren't always going to mesh, they'd taken to meeting here on the Saturday mornings he didn't have to work. Since his west-Wichita house was nearer than LeeAnn's east-side apartment, he generally got here first to grab a table.

LeeAnn was always right behind him, though. He'd only been there five minutes when she bustled through the door in her jeans and fancy boots, leaving behind a trail of perfume and admiring glances. That feminine confidence was the first thing that had attracted Ethan to her, with her well-toned body coming in a very close second. She worked hard to stay fit.

"It's great to see you, Ethan." She leaned down to press a kiss against his lips before settling in across from him. "I hope I didn't keep you waiting."

"Of course not."

As she studied the menu, *he* studied *her*. Her beaded Western shirt and gold necklace showed off a great tan—another thing she maintained diligently. As usual, she appeared to be ready to rope the world and make it hers. "You're lookin' good this morning," he said.

Glancing up, LeeAnn winked at him. "You are, too. You hungry? I can't do a whole order of French toast, but it sounds good. Have half and order another entrée for yourself."

Ethan considered her offer. Sometimes, they ate breakfast here and went their separate ways, meeting again in the evening when they were both free. Whenever they could manage it, they had a big breakfast and spent a long, leisurely day together. This morning, neither of those options sounded interesting.

Ethan's mind kept returning to Callie. Seeing her had thrown him back in time. However, instead of recalling the turmoil that had finally ended their marriage, he'd kept remembering the good times. He'd forced himself to get through the week without driving out to Augusta to see her again.

He dragged his thoughts back to the pretty woman sitting across from him, awaiting an answer.

"Sorry, LeeAnn. I'm not up for this," he said. "Do you mind if we just get coffee or juice? Tonight after your show, we can do anything you want."

"Biscuits and gravy don't sound good?" she asked, naming a Beacon specialty he normally found irresistible.

"Not really."

After they'd ordered their drinks, LeeAnn leveled a gaze at him. "Still thinking about last Saturday?"

"Maybe," he said. Since he prided himself on his honesty, he corrected himself immediately. "Yes."

"I can't believe you didn't tell her."

"You've said that," Ethan said. "I don't know why it matters when I tell her. I will. I don't want to just dump it on her."

"You've said that," LeeAnn said, winking again as the waitress brought their drinks.

"Any reason we should hurry?" he asked.

"I don't know, Ethan. What do you think?"

Aha! LeeAnn was losing patience with him. Why didn't he feel flattered at her eagerness to take the relationship to the next level? He'd thought he was ready, too.

From the beginning, he'd been honest with LeeAnn. He'd told her that he was still married, but that he'd reconcile with his wife when hell froze over. He still believed that to be the truth.

Callie owned a piece of his heart, but she'd been impossible to live with in the end.

He liked LeeAnn. She was outgoing, sophisticated and pretty in a vivid, brunette way. Basically, she was everything Callie wasn't. But as Ethan watched her drink her glass of orange juice, he noticed the way she held it with a light touch and sipped slowly.

Why, all of a sudden, did he find it sexier for a woman to order what was possibly her first beer at the age of twenty-nine, hold on to it with a death grip and drink it so fast her eyes glazed over?

And why did Callie's paler features remain in his thoughts as the ideal of feminine beauty?

She'd tied him in knots. Again.

"I think you should dispatch the papers to your wife and be done with it," LeeAnn said. "She told you she didn't want you around."

Ethan smiled. He'd decide how to handle Callie. Maybe he should learn to be honest to LeeAnn without telling her every detail. "I appreciate the input," he said, turning the conversation to other topics.

Twenty minutes later, he stood and tossed a couple of bills on the table. "You ready?"

"I'm ready." LeeAnn led him from the restaurant with a sure stride. Anyone watching might think him lucky to be with her.

That was probably true. LeeAnn was terrific.

After walking her to her car, however, Ethan kissed her quickly and tried not to think of a more provocative parking lot kiss. "I'll call you later," he promised before he closed the car door between them.

In his car, Ethan sat for a minute, thinking. He hadn't told LeeAnn, but he had the day off.

He had no, business heading to Augusta.

LeeAnn was right. Callie would no doubt be thrilled if she received divorce papers. She'd sign and return them, and she'd be through with him.

As he left the parking lot and headed east out of town, Ethan tried not to think about where he was going, or why. He just switched on the radio and drove. He wound up sitting in his car at Augusta's city lake, staring at the shady clearing where he'd proposed to Callie.

He could picture the two of them, stocking the kitchen in their first Wichita apartment. They'd talked for hours about their plans. Careers in law enforcement and biomedical research. Three kids, because he'd been a lonely only and she enjoyed her sisters so much. Date nights on Saturdays and family time on Sunday afternoons.

He was a different person now.

But he was a good man, he reminded himself. This guilt was unwarranted. He hadn't left Callie to pursue a life of debauchery. He'd left after she'd made it clear that she believed her mother's tenets about men in general and about him in particular.

Damn it all, anyway.

Tomorrow, he'd pull those papers from his filing cabinet and send them to Josie's address. Callie would receive them while she was within easy driving distance. If she had problems with anything, they could meet to talk.

And after the concert tonight, Ethan would take Lee-Ann out to celebrate a new start.

That decided, Ethan drove away from the lake with every intention of heading home. But he couldn't resist driving by Isabel's house one last time, just to see which cars were parked in front of it.

And when he saw the silver Toyota truck with a JO-Z vanity plate, he had to stop.

Callie's youngest sister had been twelve when he'd met her. The last time he'd seen her, she'd been twenty-one and in her senior year of college. Rowdy and fun, Josie was the least complicated of the Blumes. Callie couldn't blame him if he dropped by to say hello to Josie.

By the time he got to Isabel's front door, he'd almost changed his mind. He knocked anyway, and his nerves about did him in until a stranger answered the door.

"If you're here to help, come on in and find where you need to be," the man said. "If you're looking for the Blumes, they're somewhere in the back of the house."

"Thanks." Ethan followed him into the living room, where the stranger and two other guys were installing new Sheetrock. On his way through the house, Ethan saw two more men ripping out the ruined kitchen flooring.

Isabel and Josie were removing old wallpaper from the top half of Izzy's bedroom, presumably intending to match it to the newly replaced bottom half.

"Knock, knock," he said. "I'm just stopping by to visit my favorite tomboy."

"Ethan!" Josie set down the paintbrush she'd been using to apply a chemical stripper, then rushed across the room to throw her arms around his neck. After a warm hug that did much to feed Ethan's courage, he backed up, smiling as he studied Callie's youngest sister.

Just below average height, voluptuous Josie had very dark, very short hair. Isabel was a couple of inches taller, with lighter brown hair and an hourglass figure. And Callie was a blonde, of course, and just four inches shorter than his own six-two. Except for similar upturned noses and full lips, the Blume sisters were all very different in appearance.

Josie glanced at the peeling wallpaper with a grave expression. "The place looks awful, doesn't it?"

"It's much improved over past weekend," Ethan said, gazing across at Isabel. "I can't believe how fast your house is coming together."

"I've had a lot of help," Isabel said, her expression as calm as usual.

He returned his attention to Josie, and recalled the one thing that the Blume girls did have in common. A quality they had each inherited from their mother—fortitude.

They wouldn't be bested by any disaster.

Callie had inherited their mother's strongest and most difficult traits. He wondered where she was today. He'd seen the little Mazda outside, but maybe one of her sisters had dropped her off at Isabel's boyfriend's place. "Is Callie babysitting again?" he asked.

"Ha!" Josie said.

"No, she's not babysitting." Isabel spoke loudly, scowling at Josie.

Josie returned the glare, then she and Izzy engaged in a sibling dispute using only their facial expressions.

Isabel must have won, because she finally turned to him and said, "The baby is spending the morning at a church day care. The two older kids are with their dad. I think they were planning to muck out the hog bins. Roger said they'd missed doing that all last week because of the flood. The smell had begun to waft all the way to the house."

Whoa! That was too much information. Ethan didn't care where the kids were and what they were doing.

He'd been fishing for information about Callie, of course, but her sisters weren't biting. They stood in the middle of Isabel's bare, torn-apart bedroom, eyeing him.

He could simply ask to speak to Callie, but this was more fun. He raised his eyebrows, shoved his hands into his pockets and waited.

A moment later, he began to whistle.

Finally, Josie said, "Aw, heck, Ethan. Callie's in the basement if you really want to see her."

"It can't hurt to say hello," he said, grinning as he set off in that direction. Walking through Isabel's house, he listened to the sounds of hammers and scrapes and murmured voices as a houseful of people worked to repair the flood damage. The place looked just as odd as it had last week, but in a different way. He'd never seen so many men inside it. When Ella was alive, she'd hired only female plumbers and electricians, and she'd done that only after she'd exhausted herself trying to fix various problems on her own.

At least Isabel hadn't followed in her mother's footsteps in that way. Thank God.

When he'd gone halfway down the basement steps, Ethan was struck again by the ravages of the flood. If the upstairs appeared odd, the basement was surreal. Every scrap of wallboard had been cleared—it must have disintegrated in the floodwater. Isabel was left with little more than a muddy cement foundation and wet wooden studs.

A couple of industrial-size fans were running on either end of the oblong space, but the basement still carried the foul odor of standing water. Ethan spotted a plastic poinsettia that had moored itself between two ceiling crossbeams, and realized the amount of work left to do here.

And that he wanted to help do it.

Today. Tomorrow. Hell, he'd even volunteer to help until Isabel's house had been restored to its preflood state. Maybe by then, he'd think of a way to talk to Callie.

She stood facing the far wall, attacking a muddy stain with a scrub brush. Her left hand was now bare.

He kept his ring in a tiny stone box in his sock drawer. He wondered what she'd done with hers. He couldn't ask, though. He couldn't handle more than the task at hand.

At the moment, he intended only to inform her that he was determined to stay and help. He tried to clump loud enough to alert her to his arrival, but the fans were too loud. He faked a cough instead.

She noticed him, then let out a raspy chuckle.

He stepped near enough to speak to her without having to holler. "Callie, you don't have to say a word to me, but I'm planning to stick around to help. Pretend I belong with the crew upstairs."

Looking stern, she dipped her brush into a bucket containing a liquid that smelled like bleach. He watched her scrub for a minute, then he took the brush from her hand and stepped in front of her to add some muscle power. The stain disappeared.

He smiled as he returned the brush, but she responded with a deeper scowl. She sidled a few feet away from him and attacked a new stain with a vengeance. After a moment, she said, "I'd have thought you'd know better than to show up here."

He would have thought so, too. But he played dumb and asked, "Because of last weekend?"

She kept working, but raised her eyebrows.

He wondered what bothered her most. Seeing him at all, knowing about LeeAnn, or that kiss in Mary's parking lot. "Don't worry about it," he said, thinking he'd cover all the bases.

"I'm not worried." She skittered across the wall two more feet. "You're the one with the girlfriend."

Aha! It was LeeAnn. "She knows I talked to you," he said. "I'm honest with her."

"Then she knows we kissed and you got hot enough to…" Callie's voice trailed off as she glanced at his groin, and her kitten-gray eyes lit with awareness.

Need shot through Ethan as fast as lightning.

He and Callie might have lost their desire for each other while their marriage was failing, but lately they weren't having any trouble finding it.

He watched her as she resumed her scrubbing. She wore light blue sweats, her hair was pulled into a sloppy ponytail and her bare face shone with the sweat of her work.

This woman appeared to reside in a different world from the perfectly dressed, perfectly poised woman Ethan had left this morning in Wichita.

Most men would go for LeeAnn in a heartbeat.

Most would avoid a shy, workaholic scientist who believed that men were worthwhile only on a short-term basis.

But Callie intrigued him more.

Damn.

He couldn't do it again. He had tried and he had failed.

"Don't worry about my reaction to you," he said, his tone gentle. "It's probably normal to think about your first love that way. It doesn't necessarily mean anything."

Callie kept scrubbing. After a minute, she turned to peer at him.

"You want to help?" she asked.

"Sure."

She handed him the brush. "Have a blast," she said. "But get your Dudley Do-Right thrills out of your system this morning, okay?"

After nudging the bucketful of cleaner toward him with her foot, Callie jogged up the stairs.

Chapter Four

Making a beeline for Isabel's bedroom, Callie strode inside, yanked the door closed behind her and stood leaning against it. "Did you guys talk to Ethan?" she whispered to her sisters.

Josie peeled off a long strip of wallpaper, dropped it into a wastebasket and swiveled around. "Sorry. I'm the one who told him you were downstairs."

"Neither of you mentioned Luke, did you?" Callie asked.

Isabel glanced over her shoulder. "I said he was at the church day care, but I implied he was there because Roger was busy. Don't worry. Your secret is safe."

"Thanks." Callie relaxed against the door. "I'll need your help again in a few minutes. I'm supposed to get Luke from the church at one o'clock, so Ethan has to be gone before then."

"You really should tell him, Cal." Josie's hazel eyes were unusually serious as she stepped closer.

"Why?"

She rolled her eyes. "Because Luke is his kid."

Callie sighed and shook her head. Every time they'd discussed how to handle Ethan, she and her youngest sister had had this same debate. But Josie had never gone beyond casual dating. She hadn't been around kids much. Either she didn't understand Callie's dilemma, or she chose to ignore it. "And what will happen if I tell him?" Callie asked.

"Ethan will know he's a dad."

"I live in Denver," Callie said, knitting her brow. "Ethan lives in Wichita, and he's the one who left me, remember? Do you want your nephew to wonder which place is home? Ethan might even win full custody. He is Luke's biological dad, and a well-liked police officer. Do you want me to lose Luke?"

"Of course not."

"We were fine without our dad," Callie pointed out.

"Maybe, but at least our dad had a choice."

"And what did he choose, Josephine Sarah?"

Josie rolled her eyes again, and Callie let out a low growl of pure frustration. "Just help me," she insisted.

Josie returned to her work without commenting, but then Isabel turned around. "Callie, we'll do what we can, but please open the bedroom door now. The last thing any of us needs is to pass out from these chemical fumes."

"Good. Okay. Thanks," Callie said to Isabel.

She opened the door, but she glared at Josie's back for a few moments before she stepped into the hallway. Then she checked her watch. It was just after eleven o'clock. She'd give Ethan an hour.

Until that time, she wanted to be alone. In a house with people working in almost every room, that was difficult. She finally locked herself in the bathroom to scrub the tub. The water had seeped up through the pipes, leaving behind a thick layer of grime and rust.

Poor Isabel. Reminding herself that she was here for her

sister, who must be tiring of the interruptions to her life, Callie concentrated on her work for exactly sixty minutes. Then she headed for the basement stairs. On the way, she heard Ethan's voice. He must have come upstairs to help the crew of buddies Josie had invited here to help today. Callie altered her course. As soon as she'd located him in the kitchen, she said, "Ethan, may I speak with you?"

"Hang on."

She watched him work with the two other guys to yank up a piece of flooring. Ethan had knelt down to run a crowbar beneath a strip of linoleum.

Callie tried to ignore his bulging thigh and arm muscles.

After a few seconds, all three men grabbed an edge and lifted slowly. A loud ripping sound filled the room, and the flooring came loose. The men cheered, then Ethan stood and walked across the room to Callie. "What is it, babe?"

His expression was relaxed, his tone *intimate*. Had he forgotten their separation? Callie scowled and asked him to follow her out to the front porch.

As soon as they were outside, she crossed her arms in front of her. "Babe?"

"I wondered if you'd caught that." Ethan stepped down onto the top porch step, then copied her frosty stance. "It was just a slip. Don't worry about it."

"A slip."

"Don't pick a fight, Callie. I just forgot, okay? Why did you bring me out here?"

"It's time for you to go."

"I have the day off. If Josie's friends can stick around to help, I can, too. And I know they're staying all day because they told me they were."

"They were never married to me or my sisters."

"My presence here can't hurt a thing."

"Oh, but it can."

"For Pete's sake, Cal. You've actually gotten grouchier. I'd have thought you'd be over all that by now."

"Over all what?"

He studied her mouth, then her eyes. "The sadness," he said. "I understood it after your mom died, and our problems getting pregnant compounded things, but after a time you have to accept the things that happen and go on."

If only it were that easy. In a four-year time span, she'd dealt with infertility, her mother's passing and the failure of her marriage. Luke's birth had made her feel okay again.

"Believe me, I know that," she told Ethan now.

"Good. Are you happy?"

She thought of Luke. Of the exquisite feel of his head when she tucked it under her chin and rocked him to sleep. Of the overpowering warmth that filled her when he wrapped his sturdy little arms around her neck.

Of the ultimate sweetness of her little boy.

"In a lot of ways, I'm happier than I've ever been," she said.

Ethan stepped nearer. "You don't act happy when you're around me. You must still be angry with me," he murmured. "Surely you know you pushed me away."

She did know. She'd been awful to Ethan. She'd been shrewish about so many things, and when he'd talked about returning to Kansas so he could accept a spot on Wichita's helicopter patrol, she'd been furious with him for not recognizing the importance of her work in Denver.

She'd wanted him to stay. She'd hoped he would keep putting up with her moodiness. She'd needed to know she was worth that much to him.

Callie searched her brain for wise words, but found

none. She'd just opened her mouth to change the subject when the door opened behind her.

She felt pushes and jabs from several sharp limbs as the entire renovation gang piled onto the small porch. She scooted to the side, allowing them to pass.

"There you are," Isabel said as she emerged last and locked the door behind her. "If you can't tell, we're leaving." She caught Callie's eye and lifted a single brow, sending a message that this was her way of helping.

Josie and most of the guys were already at the curb. Some were climbing into a big white sedan, and others into Josie's truck.

The nice-looking blond man, Josie's good friend Gabriel Thomas, stayed behind. "Hey, buddy," he said to Ethan. "We're all going to the Hilltop Church. Isabel says they're serving chicken and dumplings to flood victims and helpers. Let's grab some grub, then we can tackle that floor again."

Callie scowled. Without waiting for Ethan's response, she said, "Ethan is heading home."

"But I didn't eat breakfast," he said, "and I did help. Didn't I, Isabel?"

Isabel glanced at Callie and shrugged. "He did."

"That settles it," Gabriel said. "Let's go."

The two men walked away. Gabriel squeezed into Josie's truck while Ethan got into his car.

Callie watched the vehicles disappear down the street. Then she gaped at Isabel. "How did that happen?" she asked.

"I don't know," her sister said, "but I imagine people deal with this sort of problem whenever they tell a whopping lie."

Isabel rarely stuck her nose into the middle of a dispute, and Callie didn't like it. She sighed. "Izzy, Ethan left when we were trying to get pregnant. He chose not to have a baby with me."

"He *has* a baby with you. He just doesn't know it."

"We don't have time to discuss this. What if Ethan is still there when it's time for me to get Luke from the church nursery?"

"The nursery is in a different part of the building," her sister said. "It'll be all right. You'll see."

Minutes later, Callie drove toward the church, allowing Isabel to travel ahead of her. She arrived last and parked her rental car at the far end of the lot so Ethan couldn't easily peek inside and discover Luke's car seat.

She hoped the gang would get their food and take their seats before she arrived at the meal hall. She wanted to sit as far away from Ethan as possible.

Unfortunately, as soon as she walked inside, she saw him standing in the church vestibule. "You should have gone on through the line," she muttered as she strode past.

"I thought we'd finish our conversation over lunch," he said, catching up to her.

"I don't think so."

After she'd filled a tray with a delicious-smelling bowl of chicken and dumplings, a glass of iced tea and a thick slice of apple pie, Callie approached Isabel's table, sat down and picked up her fork.

Ethan chose a seat across from her, so she filled her mouth with a nice-size dumpling. If she pretended to be famished, perhaps she could get away with silence.

Just then, Josie walked into the area with Luke on her hip and his diaper bag looped over a shoulder. "Look who I found," she said, beaming at Callie. "Can he have one of my dumplings if I cut it into tiny pieces?"

Callie glanced at Ethan with that nice-size dumpling

sticking in her throat. She swallowed hard, then glared at her baby sister.

When Josie noticed Ethan at the table watching, her mouth popped open. She must not have realized Ethan had been invited to join them.

She'd better not have realized.

Dropping her fork with a clatter, Callie knocked over her drink, then righted it and jumped up to grab napkins from the empty places around her, dabbing at the spill. Every clumsy movement was intended to take Ethan's attention away from Josie and Luke.

But peacemaking Isabel saved the moment. She stood up and reached for Luke. "Come here, doll face," she said as she cuddled him against her chest. "Tell silly Josie that you'd love to try a dumpling, and that you have four teeth to chew it with."

Ethan watched it all with shrewd brown eyes.

He wasn't just a cop because he got a kick out of helping people. He was a detective sergeant because he was sharp.

"Did you say how long you've been dating Roger, Izzy?" he asked.

Isabel studied him. "I've known Roger for a little over two years, but we haven't always dated in the strictest sense of the word."

"But he's your boyfriend?"

"I guess so."

"That's it, then!" Ethan nodded. "That's why you girls are acting funny."

"Why?" Callie asked.

"Luke is yours, isn't he?" Ethan said.

Callie panicked until she realized that her estranged husband had addressed *Isabel*.

Not her.

He'd guessed wrong again, thank God. Callie glanced around, checking to see who had noticed his error. Josie had filled her mouth with food and was chewing as if her life depended on it. Isabel held Luke and watched Callie for cues. The other guys had started eating at the next table, and weren't paying attention.

Callie drew in a deep breath and slowly let it out.

"If you've been seeing Roger for two years, the baby would have to be yours," Ethan told Isabel. "How old is he? Almost a year, right? A guy in my unit has a baby that age."

Callie sat back in her chair, stifling a laugh that would almost certainly sound maniacal.

Ethan smiled at Isabel. "He's a handsome kid," he said in a reassuring tone. "These days, a lot of women have babies before they marry. Let me know if you want me to talk to your Roger about doing the right thing."

"Oh, no. That's not necessary," Isabel said quickly.

And finally, *mercifully,* everyone began to eat their chicken and dumplings.

Wow. Callie should be ecstatic. But as she sat with her tea-dampened blouse sticking to her skin, she realized she didn't feel good about her narrow escape. She was relieved, of course. But she also felt as if someone had held her by her feet and shaken her violently, so that her heart was bruised and overworked.

She needed quiet.

She excused herself and got up. After explaining to her sisters that she'd return in a few moments, she left the dining area.

Luke started fussing, but Callie fisted her hands and ignored him, as much as it hurt. She strode toward a darkened hallway and didn't stop until she found a vacant Sunday-school room.

She felt like crying, too, dammit.

This was all so hard. Her sisters might not realize it, but she didn't particularly want to lie to Ethan. She hated deceiving a man who'd been wonderful to her for eight years.

But she had to live her life. And she wanted to feel as if the future belonged to herself and her baby boy.

She understood why Ethan had made the assumption he had about Luke. They'd tried hard to get pregnant, and he'd been with her the last time she'd had a blood test that had proved she wasn't. He'd known about the preserved embryos, of course, but he wouldn't have expected Callie to try again.

Ethan's belief that Luke was Isabel's child could only be a temporary fix. He lived and worked in Wichita, just twenty-some miles from her sisters. The city was huge and growing every year, but Isabel had run into Ethan at Christmastime.

Josie worked in Wichita, too. If she saw Ethan, she might decide that truth was a nobler cause than loyalty. Even if she didn't, who knew how much time would pass before something else happened?

Ethan hadn't visited her sisters in the last couple of years, but he might. He'd notice Luke's absence and ask questions.

This situation had grown far too complicated.

Callie sat in a folding chair, willing Ethan to finish eating and leave, whether he returned to Isabel's house or went home to Wichita. She had to think of a way to convince him to leave her and her sisters alone forever, just as their father had done.

No divorce. No communication. No threat.

A nearly impossible task.

"What's wrong?" Ethan asked from the hallway behind her.

She wasn't surprised. He'd been following her around an awful lot since last Saturday. "I wanted a minute alone."

He walked in and sat one row behind her and two seats down. "It's tough, huh?"

"You don't know the half of it."

"I understand more than you think," he said. "Isabel had a baby when she wasn't ready for one, and you tried so hard and were left with a nursery full of unneeded furniture."

Callie sighed and closed her eyes. Hiding the truth had become exhausting. It might be easier to tell him and deal with his reaction.

"The solution is simple," he said.

"How so?"

"Stop giving in to your fears, Cal. Put yourself out there again and you might have better luck with the next guy." He added gently, "I've moved on, with LeeAnn."

That wasn't at all what she had expected to hear.

She might feel horrible about keeping the truth from Ethan, but she didn't feel bad about protecting her son from some woman she didn't know—some no doubt flashy musician who didn't mind dating a married man.

What if Ethan married LeeAnn? Some judge might see that the child's biological father had settled down again, and that he hadn't done anything wrong. That judge might decide Ethan should be the custodial parent.

Callie's heart skittered at the thought.

"You really should begin dating again," Ethan said. "I know you treasure your independence, but the right man will only enhance your life."

In the quiet Sunday-school room, the scraping of Ethan's chair legs against the floor echoed. He stood, stepped between the rows of chairs and knelt in front of her. Callie didn't know his intentions, but her body responded to his nearness with a stinging ache, her heart with a quickening rhythm.

Ethan rested his hands on her thighs and leaned forward, surprising her by gazing into her eyes. She saw something in his expression that shook her up even more.

Compassion, yes. He'd been good at that. And desire. She was glad to have affected him, too. But there was something else. Something deeper and more solid.

An unselfish wish for her well-being?

Whatever it was, she wanted to bottle it and carry it around with her, taking it out again whenever she wanted to relive the sunny warmth of it.

His kiss stunned her.

It was short and sweet—a farewell kiss. But then he nudged her knees apart and slid his body forward, opening his mouth to hers again.

If last week's kiss had been seductive, this one was tempestuous. As his tongue plunged against hers, he pressed his hands against the small of her back to bring her hips forward.

Sweet heaven.

She'd thought she'd live the rest of her life without feeling those hands gliding against her skin. Those lips, making her feel both needed and needful at the same time. She'd thought she'd die without ever feeling this staggering heat again.

Before she accepted her lonely fate, Callie allowed herself to absorb the experience one more time. She'd just entertained the thought of tugging Ethan's shirt off when she heard whispers.

She opened her eyes, pulled her face away from her husband's and rotated in her seat.

A middle-aged man and woman were standing in the

doorway, holding several bags of groceries. "Excuse us," the man said. The couple scurried past and left the bags on a table at the front of the room. Then, as if they were the ones out of place, they exited quickly.

Callie turned around. Ethan was standing again and frowning, as if deep in thought.

She stood, too.

She'd messed up. Let her heart rule. She'd have to work extra hard to convince him that…what? That she hadn't encouraged that kiss? That she didn't want to lock the Sunday-school room door so they could make out as if they were teenagers again?

That she wasn't a fool woman who still had a thing for the husband who'd left her?

After a few seconds, Callie asked, "What did that kiss prove, exactly?" Her voice sounded sober enough, but her cheeks and body were flaming.

Ethan looked a little pink, too. "I don't know. Maybe that you're missing something."

"With you?" She forced herself to breathe normally.

Ethan eyed her for a minute, as if wrestling with some decision. "With another man," he finally said. "If you still want a baby that badly, you're going to have to get involved again. Right? It seems to me that we'd both benefit from a divorce."

Finally, he left the Sunday-school room. By the time she had made her way to the church dining hall, he was gone.

He probably thought she'd gotten her way, as usual, but of course she hadn't.

She could never have her way again.

ALMOST A WEEK LATER, Callie watched Luke pat his chubby hands against the water in Josie's sink. "You enjoy water, don't you, Lukey?" she asked, smiling.

Luke splashed harder, as if he'd comprehended the question and wanted to prove his mama right. He understood so much more, lately. Callie wondered if he'd have some fragment of memory about the weeks he'd spent with his Kansas aunts. He thrived under their affection. He'd even begun to adapt to the changed environment.

So had Callie. Although she checked in with her Bio-Labs supervisor several times a week, probing for details about the research trials, she couldn't neglect her little sister for a career. Her lab assistants were handling the exhaustive data collection tasks. She'd want to direct the interpretation of the information, of course, but for now she felt as if she was right where she belonged.

She also wondered if Luke would have any memories of Ethan. When she was in the hospital with Luke after he was born, Callie had decided that she would tell him the truth—that he was conceived in a special way because she'd had problems getting pregnant, but that she wanted him very much and couldn't love him more.

Now she wondered if she should say something about his father. He'd probably ask, at some point. He might want to know at least one of his biological parents.

Callie wished she could ask her mother for advice. Ella had raised three girls without help. After their father had left, she'd just continued on as if he'd only been meant to be a part of their lives for a short time. His departure hadn't broken her stride.

Callie hadn't only broken stride after Ethan's departure, but she'd flirted with major depression. Her pregnancy had kept her going. And now Luke did.

Her little boy shrieked. He had stuck his finger into the faucet, causing a wild spray of water to soak half the kitchen.

"No, punkin'. You're getting me wet," she said, smiling as she nudged his hand away from the flow of water.

Luke wrinkled his nose and snickered.

"You ornery thing," Callie said with a chuckle. "Let's get you dressed so I can fix dinner for your aunts."

She picked up Luke and cradled him against her as she opened the sink stopper. Grabbing a fluffy towel from the counter, she wrapped it around her baby and patted him dry before hustling him through to Josie's living room, which currently served as her and Luke's temporary bedroom.

Laying Luke on the middle of the sofa, she diapered him. He liked being naked almost as much as he liked being wet, so she'd learned to work fast and keep talking. "When we get home, I'll enroll us in one of those 'Mommy and Me' swim classes," she said as she wrestled his kicking legs into a pair of overalls. "What do you think of that?"

He grinned and grasped a buckle. "Ga."

Callie chuckled. When she spoke to Luke, he usually answered her in one way or another. They had an amazing bond. She hoped they always would.

After tugging a tiny T-shirt over his head, she buckled the overall straps and picked him up. "There you go, all dressed," she said on her way to the kitchen again.

After easing him onto the floor, out of her work path, she pulled a red melamine mixing bowl and wooden spoon from the cabinets. She beat on the bottom of the bowl once, and then handed both bowl and spoon to Luke.

He tipped the bowl over, inserted the spoon and made stirring motions that clacked against the sides and made him cackle at his own cunning.

Chuckling, Callie crossed to the sink to tidy the area.

When the phone rang, she grabbed it and leaned against the counter to talk to Stan, her supervisor at BioLabs. She suspected that he hadn't really called long distance to ask her how things were going with Isabel's house, and his subsequent complaints about Callie's lab assistants proved her right. The troubles he described might be management headaches, but they didn't pose a threat to Callie's research. She told Stan about a little trick she used when scheduling lab hours, and hung up feeling better.

He might have been fishing for news of her return, but she couldn't give him an answer. She didn't know how much longer she'd be in Kansas. Probably at least another month.

Callie was proud of her sisters for growing into such caring adults, but she knew their odd childhood had affected them. After spending their early years tucked away in the country trusting only one another, they found it hard to depend on other people. Especially men. How many times had Ella told them that men were untrustworthy?

Of course, they'd all since realized that Ella's emotional health had been questionable, but Callie knew it was tough for Isabel to welcome workmen into her house every day. Having Josie and Callie around eased the situation.

The doorbell rang, and Callie sighed. So much for cleaning the kitchen. She glanced at Luke. He was content with his bowl and spoon, but she wouldn't risk leaving him here alone for longer than a few seconds. She scooped him up and went to answer the door.

It was a mail carrier. "I have a package here that's too big for the slot," she said, handing a bundle of mail to Callie that included a large manila envelope.

Callie had always considered herself more thinker than

feeler, but the nape of her neck tingled. She wondered if this mail contained significant news.

"Thanks," she said before closing the door. Returning to the kitchen, she put Luke on the floor again, then slid the rubber band off the bundle and sorted through it.

The large package had originated from a west-Wichita post office. Callie's name was typed on the label. She hadn't admitted it to Ethan, but she'd kept track of him, too. He lived in a newer Wichita neighborhood, west of Maize Road. She wondered if he'd sent this.

Tears pricked her eyes when she opened the envelope and a single word isolated itself from all others on the top page.

Divorce.

Callie's worst fears were being realized. Ethan had sent divorce papers. She leaned against the counter and tried to read the note he'd included, but her trembling became too violent. Swearing under her breath, she turned around and dropped the papers on the counter, then rested her palms on either side of them to try again.

He'd asked her to meet him at his attorney's office next Thursday to discuss any additional requests she might wish to make.

A baby hand patted her leg. Luke had crawled over to pull himself up using her calf. He'd be walking soon.

He might never know his father.

Callie had known that. Had counted on it, in fact. But the divorce papers made the possibility sink in. Her little guy might never know his father—who was, at heart, a fine person. The kind of dad any little boy would be lucky to have in his life.

Luke couldn't have his dad in his life partly because she had failed—would always fail—when it came to relationships with men.

Callie's eyes grew too watery for her to continue reading. When she was trying to get pregnant, the fertility hormones had intensified her responses, but these on-the-surface emotions weren't normal for her.

She picked up her son and held him close, patting his bottom as if to comfort herself by comforting him.

"Dat!" Luke said, bouncing in her arms and pointing toward Josie's pantry. In just a couple of weeks, he'd learned that good things came from behind those doors.

Callie chuckled. Cuddling Luke *had* helped. Opening the pantry doors, she grabbed a box of animal crackers. Tearing off the box flap and wrapper, she handed the whole thing to Luke, then put him down again.

Picking up the documents, she studied them. The divorce petition and accompanying papers had been completed and signed by Ethan and a notary. Apparently, she wasn't required to do anything here except sign a waiver saying that she didn't object.

Ethan had proposed that they each keep what they had in their current possession. Since he'd left their home intact, taking only his clothes and personal things, his suggestion was extremely fair.

But, of course, the documents didn't account for Luke's existence. In every spot where children were mentioned, Ethan had filled in the blank with a zero, a no, or a none.

Callie glanced across the kitchen, to a baker's rack that held a container filled with pens and pencils. It'd be so easy to just sign that waiver, stick the documents in the mail and tell Ethan that next week's meeting in the attorney's office was unnecessary.

She'd be finished.

Maybe.

Callie had no experience with divorce and didn't know

the procedures. If an attorney scrutinized the details, she might get herself into trouble. Denver birth records must be easy to check, and she had listed Ethan as the father.

He'd be so angry. So hurt. She might inspire the court's disapproval, as well. Even her career could be jeopardized, if her colleagues or bosses learned of her deception. Her choices here might have a profound effect on her and her son's futures.

The bang of the apartment door interrupted Callie's thoughts, and soon Josie entered the kitchen. "Hey, Cal," she said, dropping her keys into a pottery bowl.

As Callie greeted her sister, she hid the papers behind her on the counter. Callie wanted to think this through before she discussed it with anyone. But what should she do with the papers? She didn't want to leave them on the counter or call her sister's attention to them, so she turned her back to Josie, rolled the papers into a coil and slipped them beneath her arm. She'd hide them in her luggage alongside her wedding band.

Josie had crouched down to greet Luke, but now she peered at Callie. "You okay?" she asked with a smile. At Callie's blank look, she cast a glance around the kitchen.

Callie had left Luke's bath soap and shampoo next to the sink, along with the pile of clothes he'd worn before his bath. And she hadn't started dinner.

"I'm just slow today," she said as she inched toward the door. "I'll get dinner going in a minute. How was work?"

"What?" Josie sounded confused.

Callie kept moving forward, but slowly. As if she was headed somewhere, but not in any real hurry and not for any important reason. "How was work?" she repeated.

Josie scowled and stood up, blocking Callie's path. "What's going on? You never ask me that."

"I don't?"

"No. You tell me what Luke did today. You talk about what's happening at Isabel's house. You don't ask me about my job. Not lately, anyway."

Was she that self-absorbed? Callie loved Josie. She was thrilled by her success. She didn't tell Josie that often, though.

Good heavens. She was far too much like their mother. Callie and her sisters had had to jump through hoops to earn Ella's praise. Passing the equivalency exams for students of their age hadn't been good enough—their mother had pushed them to master the next level. They'd been excellent students, but they'd missed much of the fun of childhood.

Callie didn't want to be so closed. Not with Luke or with her sisters. Despite Josie's resilience, having long-term houseguests couldn't be easy for her. Her apartment was crowded, and her busy social life had been temporarily throttled. She liked beer and televised sports, and often invited a gang over for impromptu parties. She could hardly do that with Luke's crib set up in her living room, and her sisters' things occupying her entire apartment.

"Sorry," Callie said. "I've been worried about everything else going on, but I am very proud of you."

Josie waved off the compliment, but not before Callie had noticed her tiny, startled smile.

Then Josie peered at the papers under Callie's arm. "What is that you're trying to hide?" she asked.

Callie couldn't conceal them now, but she could hide her thoughts of deception until she decided how to handle this. Tugging the papers out, she unrolled them and held them up for her sister to see.

"You're filing for divorce?" Josie asked.

"No."

Josie's eyes widened. "Oh. *He's* filing." She came across and took the papers. "Ethan's got these all filled out, doesn't he?" she said as she scanned them. "Hey. If you just sign in the appropriate places, maybe Luke's existence will slip right past the courts."

"Think so?" Callie asked.

As Josie stared at her, those wide eyes spoke volumes. "Could you live with yourself?"

Callie didn't answer. She didn't know. As it was, she managed to forget the mess of her life only part of each day. She always came to a moment, usually when she was lying in bed trying to sleep, when worry overtook all other thoughts. She needed to get Isabel's house cleaned and get away. Even then, she'd have to find a way to handle this new story about Isabel being Luke's mother.

"So what are you going to do?" Josie asked now, frowning as she looked up from the paperwork.

The complication had already necessitated a change in plans. Callie and her sisters had decided that Ethan shouldn't talk to the work crews, now that he believed Luke was Isabel's child. He might be able to work around a bunch of guys and never mention children who belonged to Isabel's boyfriend. Why would he? He'd met Roger only once, briefly.

But he might mention Isabel's baby to a group of men who were working on her house. Josie's buddies knew that Isabel was single and childless. Some of the hired workers might know, too. Callie would be foolish to try to corral a bunch of men to explain the situation.

Her deception was spiraling into something so complex, sometimes she doubted that she'd be able to think her way through it.

She'd eventually have to deal with the other aspect of this ruse. She'd go home with Luke. Isabel would stay here. Ethan might bump into her sister and query Luke's absence.

But Callie would deal with that problem after she'd put some physical distance between herself and Ethan.

Callie thought about Ethan and Luke, wishing for something she dreamed about, sometimes.

Then she thought about Ethan's friend, LeeAnn. She'd be pushing Ethan to divorce quickly so she could move in with a clear conscience, wouldn't she?

Memories of a couple of electrifying kisses also flashed through Callie's mind. She recalled that wonderful warmth coming from Ethan in the church Sunday-school room. That strong sense of goodwill.

Whatever his feelings for LeeAnn, Ethan must still feel something for her, too. Something warm and alive.

Maybe her jealousy skewed her thinking, but she didn't think Ethan was serious about LeeAnn. If he was, he wouldn't kiss Callie the way he had, would he? He might be persuaded that he didn't need to hurry with this divorce. Shouldn't they all concentrate on Isabel's recovery now? Ethan did care about her sisters.

Callie's confidence returned. She felt as sure and strong as she had the morning after she'd comforted three-month-old Luke through a high fever. She'd awakened later than usual that day, and panicked at the quiet until she'd discovered Luke calm again.

This would work out all right, too.

It wouldn't be easy. But it would work out.

Gathering Luke's clothes and bath items, Callie hid a smile. "Leave those on the counter when you finish looking at them," she told Josie. "I guess I'm just going to have to find another way to handle this."

Chapter Five

Pulling into the parking lot at Yia Yia's Restaurant in east Wichita, Ethan circled around, hunting for an empty spot. He let out a surprised oath when he spotted the little Mazda parked in the last row. After claiming the space next to Callie's, he exited his car. "You're already here?" he asked as soon as his estranged wife opened her car door.

"I said I'd be here at eight-thirty." She stepped out and glanced at her watch.

He was late. He hadn't hurried because he'd been certain that *she'd* be late. Wasn't she always? "Sorry," he said, feeling strange about the reversal of roles.

Callie was pretty tonight—more than pretty. Yia Yia's was upscale, so of course she'd dress up. Tonight's leaf-green dress was perfect for a warm spring evening, but the wild pattern and midthigh length were too deliberately flirty for Callie.

And yet the style suited her. Ethan wondered how she could have changed so much after only two years. "You're stunning," he said, taking care not to growl his words. "Is the dress new?"

"It's Josie's," she said, glancing down. "I didn't bring dressy clothes. You're pretty snazzy, yourself." Her eyes traveled across his chest, lingering just long enough to remind him of their lazy weekend mornings in bed.

She'd been wont to run her fingertips along his bare chest as they talked about anything and everything—until neither had wanted to talk anymore.

Sweet mercy. The memory was old, but the feelings it evoked were fresh and astonishing. Thinking about Callie that way, on this evening of all evenings, was a big mistake. They were here to talk about the divorce.

That was all.

Ethan swallowed. "Well. Let's go in."

He held the door open for Callie and spoke with the hostess, but his mind remained on his wife and her changes. He realized seconds after they were seated that she hadn't brought the divorce papers in with her. Her bag was too small to hold much more than her keys.

When she'd called to ask for this meeting, she'd said she wanted to speak to him without an attorney present. Her choice of restaurants might be considered strange, but they'd both always liked Yia Yia's, so he hadn't minded.

He'd assumed that she wanted to talk about something in those papers, but she hadn't dressed for that conversation. As she sat studying the menu and smiling mysteriously, she didn't appear to have come with the *intent* to discuss those papers.

But, hell, he needed to talk about them.

After he'd sent them, he'd had to resist tackling the mail carrier to retrieve them. "You okay, Cal?" he asked. "I mean, about the divorce packet? I hope it wasn't too big a surprise."

"I'm fine," she said, her smile fading. "I didn't expect to receive something like that in the mail, but I suppose I should have."

"It's time, don't you think?"

She didn't answer. She gazed at him for a moment longer, then returned her attention to the menu. "Do you know what you're going to order?" she asked.

Their friendly young waitress waved at Ethan on her way past, and he decided Callie was right. They could talk after they'd ordered.

Except for the shock of seeing the papers, Callie shouldn't be too upset. He'd been fair in his division of property.

He flipped open his menu and grew hungrier as he studied it. "Everything sounds good," he said. "I haven't been here since the last time we came together."

"You haven't?" Her eyes sought reassurance.

"No."

Her gaze fell to his smile, then she grinned. "Ah. Well, I want some grilled shrimp for an appetizer," she said. "Or should I get the crab cakes?"

"I'd go for the shrimp."

"Share an order with me?"

She hadn't just reminded him of LeeAnn.

LeeAnn reminded him of Callie every time she suggested that they split a restaurant course. Ethan smiled at Callie. "Okay, and I have to order the lobster risotto."

"Me, too."

They both chuckled as they refolded their menus. Yia Yia's was a treat for the senses, in more ways than one.

"Remember the time we sat here until closing, talking?" Callie asked as she studied the dining room lit softly with wall sconces and tabletop candles. Oversize booths abutted the room's limestone walls, while cloth-covered table groupings filled its center. "We wound up walking by the river afterward, and when we finally drove home to Augusta the highway was almost empty."

"It was our second anniversary," Ethan said.

"Right."

Callie didn't say it, but they must both be remembering. On their first anniversary, they'd come here, too. They'd left before they finished dinner, driving straight home. They'd made love all night long.

"Those were some good times," he said.

Callie smiled, nodding as she held his gaze.

When the waitress arrived to take their orders, she said they were a cute couple and asked if they always dressed to match.

Ethan glanced down. He hadn't realized, but he'd worn a tie with a swirl pattern that almost matched the one on the green dress. "No, it's just a coincidence," he said, not bothering to confess that they weren't a couple at all.

Not anymore.

When the waitress left, he watched Callie. He wondered about her wedding ring again, and about what else might be different in her life. He didn't want to bring up the subject of that confounded divorce packet again, even though they'd met here to discuss it.

"Isabel's house is coming along," Callie said, sparing him the trouble of finding a safe topic of conversation.

Ethan hadn't gone to Augusta to help since last Saturday—he'd had to work a shift this morning—and his thoughts about the divorce had pushed Isabel's woes from his mind for a while.

Callie wouldn't be able to get away from her sister's plight. She'd work tirelessly to help Isabel so that everyone in her family could resume their normal lives.

"Have they installed the new kitchen tile yet?" he asked.

"Not yet." Callie moved her water glass to make room for the appetizer platter, which had just arrived. After the waitress left, Ethan watched Callie transfer some shrimp to two small plates and hand one across.

"What's Isabel doing about Blumecrafts?" he asked.

"I called her repeat clients and warned them about a delay in orders," Callie said. "She'll have to restock some ruined supplies, but she'll begin making the quilts again soon. They're her biggest sellers."

Callie might be the most like their mother in some ways, but Isabel lived as frugally as Ella had. "She still doesn't mind working at home?" he asked. "It'd drive me crazy."

Callie had just bitten into a shrimp. "Man, that's good," she said as soon as she'd swallowed. Then she gasped, as if she'd remembered something. "She loves being home now," she said. "Luke needs his mama around."

"Oh, right." Ethan picked up a shrimp, but didn't eat it immediately. "Will you return to Denver soon?" he asked, trying to smooth a forehead that wanted to furrow.

"Not until Isabel is in her house," Callie said. "We're going to do a lot of the basement work ourselves, and even when she's home we'll have to clean the items we salvaged. We're not even caught up with her…with *their*… laundry. Can you imagine?"

Ethan bit into the shrimp and murmured with pleasure, responding as much to Callie's answer as to the taste of the food.

At one time, she'd been almost obsessed with her BioLabs job. He'd tried to talk her into looking for a similar position in Wichita, but she'd confused the issue, saying he didn't find her work important. He'd only wanted her to live a whole life. He'd made friends in Denver, but reticent Callie had contented herself with her research, her efforts to conceive, and him.

Maybe his absence had been good for her. Maybe she was reaching out more now.

He continued talking to Callie as they finished the appetizer, as he drank another glass of Chardonnay and as they savored their dinners. The conversation flowed from comments about the food to another discussion of Isabel's house to their jobs.

He completely forgot, until she was standing right beside him, that LeeAnn had said she'd join him after her concert.

He checked his watch. It was only ten o'clock. River's Bend must have finished early.

LeeAnn was in full regalia. Her blue jeans were slung low beneath a rhinestone-studded Western shirt and finished off with her baby-blue cowboy hat and boots.

She stood smiling at him. Callie sat scowling at her. And Ethan swiveled his gaze between the two of them. He felt extremely uncomfortable, and not only because he'd forgotten to tell Callie that LeeAnn might be joining them.

If the truth were known, he was reluctant to end his private conversation with his wife.

Estranged wife.

Soon-to-be *ex*-wife.

His feelings for Callie might be complicated, but the divorce discussion was necessary. They hadn't lived together for two lonely years. That was too long to live as he had—as an ignorant fool who didn't know whether he should divorce the woman he'd left.

Whenever someone asked Ethan if he was married, he wasn't sure how to answer.

I'm married, but I left my wife several years ago.

We're separated…indefinitely.

I'm going to divorce my wife, someday very soon.

He needed to take action.

"You gonna scoot over, cowboy?" LeeAnn asked. "Or should I plant my patootie right there in your lap?"

Cowboy? LeeAnn didn't call him cowboy, and she didn't speak to him in that tone. They weren't that far just yet.

However, her little show for Callie was probably normal under the circumstances.

Ethan slid next to the wall, allowing LeeAnn to plant her patootie on the bench next to him. "Callie, ah, Taylor, this is LeeAnn Chambers," he said. "LeeAnn, Callie."

Callie remembered her manners. She stood up halfway and extended her hand across the table. "Nice to meet you, LeeAnn. Ethan has spoken well of you."

"Oh, he talks about you, too, hon," LeeAnn said.

Callie would detest that condescending tone. Her narrowed eyes confirmed it: she was simmering.

If LeeAnn kept it up, Callie would eventually skewer her with her lightning-quick intellect.

Ethan scowled a warning at LeeAnn, but she was too busy watching Callie to pay much attention. "You act as if you are surprised to see me," she was saying. "I apologize if he forgot to mention that I'd be coming. We spend most of our Saturday nights together these days, so I told him I'd meet him here after your little talk."

Okay, that wasn't exactly true. After LeeAnn's pouty response to his news about this meeting, he'd promised to meet her later.

She'd insisted that he meet her *here,* later. She'd also suggested the dessert idea.

"Of course." Callie's expression remained calm, but Ethan didn't feel calm. He felt ignored and frustrated, and he didn't like LeeAnn's cattiness. Maybe she deserved to feel the scratch of Callie's claws.

"How was your little talk, anyway?" LeeAnn asked, still speaking to Callie.

That was none of her business. "Just fine," Ethan interjected. "We had a nice chat."

LeeAnn must have heard the insistence in his tone, because she shot him a sideways glance.

She switched gears, winking at him and giving Callie a look of wide-eyed innocence. "Good. Have you ordered dessert yet? I've heard raves about the menu here."

Callie was sharp. Would she realize that Ethan hadn't brought his girlfriend here?

Sure enough, Callie's gaze held his a touch too long, her eyes bright and soft. She thanked him silently for preserving the memory of this shared, special place.

Seconds later, she redirected her attention to LeeAnn. "You've heard right," she said in a gentle tone. "Dessert here is wonderful, but I can't indulge. I need to go." She lifted her tiny purse to the table and clicked it open.

What? She intended to leave without teaching LeeAnn a lesson? She *had* changed.

"What are you doing, Callie?" Ethan asked.

She shrugged. "Paying for my dinner, then leaving."

"But we haven't finished talking."

"Oh, well." She glanced at LeeAnn.

Callie was right again. They couldn't talk with LeeAnn sitting with them, listening. Ethan reached a hand across to snap Callie's purse shut. "I'll get this," he said, and when she angled her chin he shook his head. "I insist."

She slipped her purse under her arm and scooted from the booth. Standing beside the table for a moment, she shook hands with LeeAnn again and said goodbye to them both.

As Ethan watched her go, he wished he hadn't told

LeeAnn about tonight's meeting. If he and Callie could have spoken at leisure, they'd have eventually discussed the divorce packet. Surely they would.

He also wished for things he shouldn't.

For reasons he barely understood.

THE NEXT AFTERNOON, Callie sat in the passenger seat of Josie's truck, gripping the hand rest, watching the passing farm fields and thinking how quickly a life could end if even one of the other drivers on the road made a tiny error in judgment.

A quick turn. A slow one. Even a too-eager response to a green light could send cars crashing and souls flying.

Josie drove in the manner of certain teenage boys—skillfully, but with little regard for other folks on the road who might not be so quick to react, and with little regard for such inconsequential things as speed limits and traffic lights.

When her sister reached town and turned onto the main road, Callie noted the cars parked in front of Augusta's hardware store. *Thank God we made it,* she thought, even as she said, "Thank heaven, they're open."

Like many vendors along the highway, the store had received flood damage, too. The newspapers had reported that many businesses in this area had been under two feet of water during the worst of it. The hardware store owners were still recovering, but they had reopened quickly, willing to sell whatever they could. With luck, they had plenty of paint.

Josie pulled into the lot, stopped short in a front-row spot and scrambled out of her truck before Callie had relaxed her grip on the hand rest. "Wait, Josie," Callie hollered after her.

"Yo." Josie leaned down to stick her head in the window. "You're not coming in?"

"Not yet." Callie worked to unclench her muscles.

"What's the holdup?" Josie asked. "I want to get that bedroom painted this evening."

"Did you bring your cell phone?" Callie asked. She knew it was in Josie's glove box. She'd checked earlier.

Josie pointed. "It's in there."

"Can I borrow it?"

Josie sighed. "Relax, Cal. Luke just went to sleep an hour ago. He's fine with Isabel—you know she'll hover over him. During your hot date last night, she hardly ever put him down, even after he was asleep."

"That was no hot date, and I'm not calling Isabel."

"Oh. Well, go ahead and use it then," Josie said, smirking. "Should I wait?"

Luckily, Josie had no curiosity about Callie's plans for the phone. If she knew whom Callie was planning to call, she'd surely state her opinion about the conversation.

At the moment, Callie didn't want to hear that opinion. "Go on in and start them mixing the paint, Josio Andretti," she said. "I'll be right in."

She watched her sister disappear inside the store, then pulled a scrap of paper from her jeans pocket and Josie's phone from the glove box.

Last night hadn't gone well.

Callie had hoped to stimulate Ethan's good mood by talking about the old days, then convince him that the divorce could wait until a better time. She'd hoped he might even be convinced that he didn't like LeeAnn quite as much as he'd thought. But she hadn't counted on Lee-Ann's arrival, or Callie's emotional response to the interruption.

Or to the woman herself. LeeAnn was hot in exactly the way most men fancied. Sassy, with dark-fringed eyes and a flirtatiousness that Callie had never even dreamed of attempting.

She could understand Ethan's attraction to that type of woman—especially after he'd spent so much time with a wife who sometimes forgot that she *was* a woman.

It'd taken quite a bit of control for Callie to keep her cool after LeeAnn had arrived, especially when she'd realized that Ethan's *girlfriend* wasn't bringing her patootie by to say hello, then taking it away so Ethan and his *wife* could finish their little talk.

Ethan had been at fault for inviting LeeAnn.

LeeAnn was simply easier than Ethan to dislike.

Cowboy, indeed.

Sighing, Callie punched in the number written on the paper—Ethan's home number—then held her breath as the phone rang once, then again.

An image passed through Callie's mind, of LeeAnn sitting beside the phone at Ethan's house. Hat pulled low on her forehead, booted feet stretched across the coffee table, sass kicked into high gear.

She'd laugh when she saw Ethan's caller ID. She'd call out to Ethan that *J. Blume* was on the phone. She'd ask sweetly if she should grab it or if he wanted to get out of bed to answer.

For Pete's sake, it was almost three in the afternoon.

Callie had waited late to telephone Ethan, hoping to avoid exactly that possibility. Whether Ethan had spent the night with LeeAnn or not, he'd be out of bed.

Without question.

It was none of Callie's business.

None.

Callie closed her eyes and willed Ethan to answer. As she listened to another ring, she noticed Josie pass by the store's front window.

The fourth ring was interrupted. "Hullo."

Good, it was Ethan. "Hi, it's me."

"Yeah. Your sister's name is on my ID. Anything wrong?"

He sounded breathless. "Is this a bad time?" Callie asked, wincing.

"No. I just got home from work an hour ago, then I went for a run."

He'd worked a shift already? Callie smiled, foolishly happy to hear that he'd been at work all day. "Hard day?" she asked.

"Not really," he said, sounding tired. "We had sixteen call-outs, but most were just traffic related. We did get one call to a domestic, and the guy had a gun. Lord knows what would have happened, so I'm glad the idiot's in custody."

"I am, too," Callie said. "I won't keep you. I called because we didn't manage to finish our business last night."

"No, we didn't."

She sighed. "I need to ask for a favor."

"What is it?"

"You know we're rushing to get Isabel in her home. She needs to set up her workshop. We're all working so hard." Callie paused, took a breath, then said, "I can't take the time to meet with your attorney this week. I hope you understand."

"Sure I do. I'll cancel the appointment," he said, and added in a low voice, "You can just sign the papers and mail them, Cal. No problem."

That would be a problem, though—a huge one. With a couple of stamps and a signature or two, she could vastly increase her possibilities of losing Luke.

"Oh, but I think we probably do need to sit together with an attorney to make sure everything's in order," Callie said. "Can it wait a while, though?"

Until she'd had time to escape to Colorado...then until she'd moved, leaving no forwarding address.

Ethan was quiet for a long, long time. "I suppose so," he finally said. Then, "I really don't mind waiting. Let me know when you're ready."

Cheered by his brightened tone, Callie said goodbye and clicked off the phone. She returned it to Josie's glove box and went inside to help her sister carry the paint to the truck.

She spent the next couple of days helping her sisters in every way she could. While Luke slept, she cooked or cleaned or traded places with Isabel, painting or dealing with contractors to give her sister an opportunity to rest. When her son was awake, Callie took him along on errands or incorporated him into her routines.

She discovered that if she gave Luke a bucket of water, he loved to play-paint the steps of Isabel's concrete porch while Callie worked nearby, cleaning a few of the Christmas ornaments they'd salvaged.

Callie completed every task with speed and precision, knowing that if she and her sisters made constant progress, they'd finish soon. She could get Luke home to relative safety. She could also answer the complaints of her Bio-Labs co-workers. Her most trusted assistant, Patty, had worked two straight weeks of overtime. She was the most familiar with the data collection workstations, and she kept meticulous records. The rest of the crew had been grumbling about favoritism.

Callie knew her colleagues could settle the problem themselves if they focused their energies creatively, but she really should think about getting her life and her research back on track.

And if she stayed busy enough, the memories she'd refreshed during one Saturday evening at Yia Yia's wouldn't hurt quite so much.

On Tuesday, after she and Luke had spent the morning grocery shopping, Callie dropped by the house to take her sister some lunch. She gasped when she noticed Ethan's car at the curb. She glanced at Luke, who was sitting in his car seat drinking orange juice from a bottle.

Taking the little boy inside would be risky. Any moment now, Ethan might see himself in Luke's brown-eyed grin or in the determined dimples that formed in his cheeks when he attempted anything new.

She should leave.

But if she went to Josie's apartment, Ethan might drop by later and find Luke with her, anyway. She frowned, feeling awful for hiding her son. Even though the alternative might turn her life to hell.

She could head to Wichita. Maybe she'd drop by the furniture showroom where Josie worked. Her little sister might steer her toward some bargains for Isabel's house— a new mattress, maybe, or a couple of living-room chairs.

Callie wondered what story Isabel had told Ethan today. Perhaps that her baby was at the church day care or out with his "Aunt" Callie.

If Callie had been Luke's aunt, she wouldn't have seen him much. She lived too far away. She'd dote on her nephew.

Ethan would buy that story.

At the thought of seeing him again, a bubble of excitement lodged in Callie's throat.

She couldn't resist.

Callie gathered Luke and his things, and headed inside. She found Isabel and Ethan in the basement, transferring a large sheet of wallboard from one future room to another.

"Look who I brought to visit you," Callie said, hoping to prompt Isabel to reveal the status of their story before she said anything more.

"Hi, Lukey," Isabel said, sending a wide smile to Luke and a tiny wink to Callie. "Have you had a good morning with your auntie?"

Luke bounced in Callie's arms and said, "Gaga," which could be interpreted to mean just about anything. Callie was thankful that her sister was sharp enough to catch on quickly, and that her son was too young to catch on at all.

After Isabel and Ethan had leaned the wallboard against the far wall, Isabel asked Ethan to excuse her. Then she came across to take Luke from Callie. Murmuring as she carried the baby up the stairs, Isabel sounded motherly.

Callie often teased Isabel about getting attached to every child she met, but at this moment she felt lucky that Isabel was a born nurturer.

Alone with Ethan again, Callie watched him rotate his shoulders, stretching them.

"I know you're going to say you don't want me here," he said in a quiet voice. "But save yourself the trouble. I've been here all morning and no catastrophe has happened. Think of it this way—an extra pair of hands will speed the process."

He had a point.

He bent his head from side to side, working out a kink. When they were together, she'd have thought nothing of offering him a massage. He'd taught her how to find the tension and rub it with just the right amount of pressure. He'd often done the same for her.

What could one little massage hurt?

She stepped nearer. "Turn around," she said quietly.

After he had, she reached up and started rubbing his neck and shoulders.

His skin was hot, his muscles firm.

Maybe others could touch this way and keep it casual. Apparently, she couldn't. This connection of fingers to flesh felt dangerous.

Yet she couldn't stop. Didn't *want* to stop.

"Thanks," Ethan said, his husky voice shooting erotic impulses through Callie's limbs. As she kneaded through a knot, he groaned and relaxed his head forward.

Callie caught her breath, resisting an urge to press her body against the long, lean planes of his back.

When things were still good, she'd loved exploring those broad muscles. She loved his smell. His strength.

She didn't know if she nudged him around or if he'd simply turned, but then they were kissing again. He tasted like coffee today—whenever he worked more hours than he should, coffee kept him going. He also tasted dangerously hot, like languid, second-time sex in a back-of-the-bar parking lot. Or like laughter-filled bedroom sex two hours before families were scheduled to arrive for Thanksgiving dinner.

Callie let her lips linger against Ethan's, savoring memories of their time together before her mother's death. Before her infertility woes.

Before Luke.

She backed up, her heart racing. She'd done it again! In remembering all the whys, she'd ignored a few important why nots. She hadn't meant to kiss him. It was an old habit.

She opened her eyes and watched Ethan's expression

grow cool. Callie should be thankful. She needed to re-member the problems in their past, as well as the plea-sures.

But she wasn't happy to see his desire for her lessen. She'd been Ethan's first love and he'd been hers. They might have each broken a few promises, but he'd broken the biggest one.

He'd given up.

In this instant, with her mouth warm with his coffee taste and her limbs infused with his heat, she wanted Eth-an to feel regret. Before he composed himself or ruined the moment by discussing it, Callie turned around and headed up the stairs.

Let him compare her kiss to any LeeAnn might give him.

Let him feel the tiniest hint of doubt that what he was doing was right.

Let him wonder if his *leaving her at all* had been right.

Chapter Six

Ethan punched the keypad next to his garage door, then ducked through the opening. It was his first Saturday off this month, and he had a ton to do. His morning run finished, he wanted a shower. Then he was headed to Augusta again.

Contractors had finished installing the major systems in Isabel's basement—she had a new furnace and water heater—and now those basement walls could be replaced. If drywall dust and sweaty skin weren't such an appalling combination, he'd skip the shower and get going.

He rushed through it, though, and dressed quickly, too. When he went into his living room and sat in his favorite chair to put on his socks and shoes, he noticed his blinking answering machine light.

He crossed the room to the side table, touched the play button and swore. LeeAnn had called while he was showering. Her message, while phrased to sound charming, was sullied by the strained tones in her voice.

She was obviously growing tired of his neglect. She had waited an hour at the Beacon this morning, she reported, and she'd finally left to meet River's Bend for a practice session. She'd be busy all week at Wichita's annual River Festival, but she wanted to know if he was all right.

Aw, hell. He'd missed their standing Saturday breakfast date. He'd worked the last two Saturdays, but today he had no excuse. He'd simply forgotten.

Obviously, she hadn't.

He grabbed the phone, thinking he'd try her cell number, then thought better of it. LeeAnn would try to talk him into dropping by to watch her practice, then spending the day with her at the festival.

He dropped the handset in its holder. He'd contact Lee-Ann later, when he was home and after he'd showered again. He'd make up for his negligent behavior after her concert tonight.

Today, he wanted to help Isabel.

A half hour later, he drove up to the old Blume place. Both Isabel's car and Josie's truck were parked at the roadside, along with several other vehicles. However, the rental car Callie drove was nowhere in sight.

Ethan was disappointed. He'd missed her on Wednesday. Isabel had said she was babysitting Luke again.

Go figure. Ethan would have expected take-charge Callie to do more of the physical work. He'd have expected child-loving Isabel to be so involved with her baby that she'd let her sisters repair the house.

That particular role reversal wasn't a complete shocker, though. Callie also loved babies, and she was a strong woman. She hadn't let her childless state keep her from being a doting aunt. He was proud of her for that.

He'd been thinking about her more than usual lately—especially after that basement kiss. Had she noticed his arousal? After another minute or two of kissing, they might have initiated the recently dried floor of Isabel's basement. He'd have risked a return to the hellish end of their marriage for just one more time in the haven of Callie's body.

Would he ever make love to her again?

Of course not. He shouldn't even think that way. A hot early sex life hadn't protected them against the intense fighting that had torn them apart later.

It wouldn't resolve anything now.

If Ethan helped Isabel, he'd be speeding her recovery from the flood, and ergo his divorce from Callie—which was exactly what he needed to do.

Then, he'd pursue a robust sex life again, with LeeAnn or whomever else came along. Then, this drawn-out obsession with Callie would end.

He hoped.

When Josie emerged from Isabel's front door a moment later, she looked surprised to see him. She stopped on the porch step, and looked as if she might turn around and go back in. Finally, she squared her shoulders and stepped down, meeting him halfway across the lawn.

"Hi, Ethan," she said, smiling. "It's gorgeous out here today, isn't it?"

Ethan perused the dazzling blue sky and the leafy shrubs and trees in Isabel's yard. The pile of flood debris had finally been carried off by county crews, and the grass was freshly mown. "It is," he said. "If those inspector's placards weren't taped to all the doors, you might forget that this area was underwater a little over a month ago."

"Probably. Hey, give me a hand," Josie said as she crossed the yard toward her truck.

"That's why I'm here," he said as he fell into step beside her. "To help."

Josie continued across the lawn. "We've had a lot of help," she said. "Izzy will be living at home in another month. Maybe sooner."

That was true. Isabel's list of flood-related needs was

dwindling. "I heard she was ready to install wallboard in the basement," Ethan said as he watched Josie pull a tub of laundry supplies from her truck bed.

Josie balanced the container against her hip, then pointed to a small box of cleaners. "Grab that, would you?"

He did, then he followed her toward the house.

"Some of my buddies are working on those walls," Josie said on the way. "I got kicked upstairs to help Isabel with laundry." She stopped below the steps and turned around. "They won't have room for you, either."

How disappointing. "How many guys are down there?" Ethan asked.

"Eight. They're pretty cranky, too. Everyone's hot and sweaty. I'll be surprised if they don't get into a brawl before they're finished."

Considering the size of Isabel's basement, eight would be two or three too many. Ethan shifted the box to his other side and considered his options.

He should go home and get hold of LeeAnn.

"At any rate, Callie's not here," Josie said. "She took Luke to the City Park today."

Ethan might have argued that he was here to support the entire family, and not just to see Callie, but Isabel opened the door just then. "Josie, what's taking you so long?" she asked.

Then she spied Ethan. "Oh, Ethan. Um. You can't… uh…" She colored.

"We were just chatting," Josie said. "He showed up to work in the basement, but I already told him we couldn't fit one more guy down there. He's leaving."

"Oh!" Isabel's cheeks turned pinker. "Well, that's true, and I'm so sorry." She stepped outside and took the box from him. "I hope you know how much I appreciate your help."

"No problem. I should have called Josie's apartment before I drove all the way here. I have things to do at home, anyway."

"Then you're heading back to Wichita?" Josie asked.

"Yes. He is," Isabel said with uncharacteristic certainty. "See you later, Ethan. My phone service will be restored sometime this week. Call first, next time."

"Good idea. Well, bye, ladies." Ethan headed for his car.

"Because if you weren't going straight home," Josie hollered after him, "you could drop by the park to wish Luke a happy birthday."

The baby's birthday was today?

Ethan swiveled around to watch Callie's sisters, who stood on the porch glaring at each other. Neither acted as if they realized he was studying them.

Isabel murmured something about Callie being upset.

Josie responded by saying something about an insane plan.

"His first birthday?" Ethan asked, to regain their attention.

"Yes. His very first." Josie beamed as if she'd just won this silent sister-battle.

Isabel rolled her eyes, then said, "That's right. You know how it is—a doting aunt and a busy mom. Callie knew I'd want to work here today, but we're celebrating as a family later this evening. I wouldn't neglect my own son. You know that."

Not one of the Blume sisters could be considered a chatterbox, but when Isabel was nervous, she tended to prattle. She must feel guilty about working on her baby's birthday—a forgivable sin. Ethan smiled at her. "Enjoy his party tonight, and take lots of pictures."

A while later, Ethan carried a large, brightly wrapped present toward the playground equipment at City Park, near Augusta's northern tip. Kids and mothers were everywhere, but he'd spotted Callie easily.

Her long, sunlit blond hair made a stark contrast to Luke's dark, newly cropped cut as they sat together at the top of the slide. As Callie scooted forward, her laughter blended with the little boy's.

She saw Ethan when she was halfway down. Obviously startled, she came to a stop at the bottom and sat for a moment, her gaze moving between Ethan and the gift.

"Wady, it's my tuwn," the little girl at the top complained. "You hafta get off."

"Oh! Sorry." Callie hopped up with the baby and approached Ethan. "What's going on?" she asked.

"Nothing." He shrugged. "I came to offer Isabel some help with the basement, but she didn't have room for me. Josie mentioned that it was Luke's birthday." He shifted the oversize package and grinned at the little boy.

"You didn't go in?" Callie asked.

He shook his head. "No. I spoke to your sisters outside."

"Oh. Okay." She nodded toward the package. "You didn't have to do that."

"I know, but think about it," he said. "If we were a couple, I'd be his uncle, right? Technically, I am still his uncle for the time being."

Callie peered at Luke. "Guess that'd be right."

Ethan watched the little boy's face. "Hi, Luke," he said in a gentle tone. "I'm Ethan. I came to wish you a happy first birthday."

The little boy pointed at the box and said, "Dat!"

Ethan chuckled.

"I think he knows the humongous package is for him," Callie said.

"Smart kid."

"Uh-huh."

"Shall we sit somewhere?" Ethan asked. "I can't stay long, but I want to watch Luke open his present."

Callie glanced around. "How about over there?" She carried Luke away from the equipment and sat in the grass with the boy in her lap. Ethan put the package in front of them, then sat on the opposite side.

Luke patted his chubby hands against the gift, obviously content to bang on the box. He pointed to a picture of a tricycle-riding bear on the paper. "Dee?"

"It's a birthday present, Lukey," Callie said. "You have to open it."

"He doesn't know about opening gifts?" Ethan asked. "Was he too young at Christmastime, then?"

"Yes, he was."

"Then this is very exciting, isn't it?" Ethan asked. He was glad he'd driven past one of the town's few discount stores. When he'd seen the shiny tricycles, bicycles and play equipment lined up along the front walkway, he'd realized that Luke must have lost a few toys in the flood.

He hadn't been able to resist going inside to find an appropriate gift for a one-year-old. He'd figured he'd drop it by, then get on his way.

Callie's sober expression suggested that she had a world of troubles on her mind. After a minute, she bent down to Luke and showed him how to tear the paper. "See? Just rip this paper right off the box," she instructed.

The little boy caught on quickly, and soon had the package unwrapped. As Ethan gathered paper scraps and wadded them into a ball, he heard a deep intake of breath, followed by a shudder.

It was Luke. The little boy's eyes had filled, and he was beginning to whimper.

"Uh-oh," Callie said. Pulling the baby around into her embrace, she patted his bottom and smiled at Ethan. "Guess he thinks the fun's all finished."

"No, Luke. *This* is your present," Ethan said, thumping his palm against the box. "The toy inside is for you. It's a basketball and goal."

Luke pushed away from Callie and turned in her arms to stare at Ethan with soft brown eyes.

Ethan took his keys from his jeans pocket and slit the tape at the package end, hoping to heaven the basketball goal didn't require construction.

He got lucky. The plastic toy was intact, inside the box. Ethan lifted it out, then spent a little while showing Luke how to toss the ball through the hoop. "I thought you might approve of this toy," he told Luke. "The first time I saw you, you were playing with a ball."

"Ba," the baby said.

Ethan and Callie laughed, then Ethan began to retrieve the ball while Luke stood braced in Callie's arms, tossing it. After a while, Luke handed the ball to Callie and focused on Ethan. He pointed to the nearby swings. "Dat."

"You want to swing, Luke?" Callie asked.

Then Callie glanced at Ethan, still sitting across from her. "I know you have to go," she said. "If you don't mind, could you repack the toy and set the box in my passenger seat on your way past? I left the car unlocked."

"You shouldn't do that," Ethan said. He started to remind Callie that bad things happened even in small towns, but Luke interrupted.

"No, no, no," the baby said, shaking his head. He shoved away from Callie, looked directly at Ethan and pointed to the swings. "Dat."

"*Somebody's* getting cranky," Callie said, chuckling as she lifted Luke into her arms.

Luke stared at Ethan, pointed to the swings and said, "Dat-dat-dat."

Ethan chuckled and stood up, too. "No. *Somebody* just wants *me* to take him to the swings."

"You don't have to," she said. "He'll be all right as soon as you're out of sight. I promise."

Ethan reached for the baby. "Want me to take you?"

The little guy catapulted away from Callie.

Ethan pulled Luke into his arms. "This is no problem, Cal. Really. I can spare an hour."

Callie stuffed the toy and wrapping paper into the box. "I'll go put these in my car."

Ethan carried Luke to the swings. By the time he'd buckled the little boy snugly into the baby swing, Callie had returned. She stood a few feet in front of them, waiting. Ethan pulled the swing back a few feet and let go, sending the child swaying toward Callie.

Luke shrieked in delight while Callie and Ethan stood smiling at each other from opposite sides of the swing set.

Dressed in jean shorts and a white T-shirt, Callie fit in with all the other mothers in the park today, except for her luscious legs. He'd always had a thing for her legs.

They were as gorgeous as ever, but she seemed different. It was nice to see her smiling again. During those last months in Denver, she'd forgotten how to enjoy life.

"You get a kick out of Luke, don't you?" Ethan asked.

"Sure I do. He's a sweet kid," Callie said, catching Luke and letting go to keep him swinging.

Too bad she wouldn't get to watch him grow up from a closer vantage point. If she saw him only on special occasions, she'd miss so much. "You ought to move back here," Ethan said.

Callie made a wry face, then caught the swing and unbuckled Luke. Pulling him into her arms, she carried him toward the slide with Ethan following.

"Why did that suggestion bother you?" he asked.

Callie sighed, then shifted Luke to one hip so she could hang on to the ladder with one hand. "It sounded like an old, tired argument. You know I love my job in Denver."

"Of course I do. Remember me? I'm the guy who desperately wanted you to come to Kansas with me."

"You wanted the position on Wichita's helicopter squad."

No. He'd wanted both—the job and Callie.

Ethan waited until she'd gone down the slide and returned to the ladder, then he admitted, "Yes, I did. And all I'm saying is that you are very attached to your nephew. Don't you want to live nearer to Isabel?"

"Living here isn't an option for me." Callie sighed when Luke reached for Ethan, but she handed him across and walked around to wait at the bottom of the slide.

Ethan carried Luke up the ladder, and when he got to the top, he held the little boy on his lap. "I guess I never understood why you were so intense about it. I only searched for work here because I thought you should spend more time with your sisters."

"You did?"

"Sure."

"I thought you just wanted a way out."

Ethan scowled, thinking back. After her mother died, Callie had been inconsolable. She'd also been frantic for a baby and following her doctor's every recommendation, to the point where Ethan had had little say in the matter.

When she'd told Ethan, for perhaps the fifth time, that she might never have married him if she'd known she couldn't have a baby, he'd given up.

Maybe leaving her had been a mistake.

Maybe the marriage had been a mistake.

No. It hadn't.

They'd married young—Ethan had been twenty and Callie nineteen—but they'd been great together for a long time.

"Why didn't you tell me that, Ethan?"

Ethan watched Luke kick his feet against the slide. "I guess that's what happens when couples don't talk. I do regret it. We should have worked harder."

Finally, Ethan let himself slide down. During that few seconds, he listened to the baby's chortle and watched Callie's face reveal a legion of emotions.

When he got to the bottom, Ethan stood with Luke in his arms and watched Callie kiss the baby on the cheek.

Then she kissed Ethan again.

This was an innocent peck beside his mouth, but it was as powerful as any kiss they'd shared. A silent apology, certainly. Callie was telling him she believed he'd had her best interests in mind, after all.

It also felt like a kiss of forgiveness.

"YOU HAVE TO STOP kissing me," Ethan said, although the warmth in his tone communicated the opposite.

Callie studied the upward curves of his mouth and the deep dimples that matched his son's almost exactly. Then she glanced into his eyes and quickly away. She couldn't believe she had just kissed him again.

But then again, she could. She'd never lost her feelings for Ethan, but she'd learned to push them aside so she could function. Spending time with him wasn't helping.

She should be careful. Whatever affection she had for Ethan—whether inspired by a new crush or a thousand old memories—couldn't be allowed to develop further. She need only remember her son, the baby Ethan believed was her nephew, to find her resolve.

"I know. I will," she replied. "That was hardly a kiss, though. I was simply saying thanks. You're a gallant ex-husband, at times."

"I'm not your ex-husband yet."

Ethan's too-quiet voice held a challenge. Callie lifted Luke from his arms and walked away.

When she realized that Ethan was walking beside her, she said, "Well, but you will be my ex. I've seen the way LeeAnn watches you. She won't let you wait long."

What was she saying?

She might not be anxious to explore thoughts of a reconciliation, but she shouldn't mention the topic of divorce again, either. Callie wondered if her plan was too outrageous. Could she escape Ethan's interest, and also avoid a divorce?

Not at the rate she was going.

Here at this Augusta park, on a bright and sunny day, with Ethan so charming and her little birthday boy so smitten with his own father, it sounded crazy. She'd have to try harder.

For the moment, she could avoid her memories and any serious discussions about their marriage, their divorce and the amazing LeeAnn.

Heading for the merry-go-round, Callie climbed on and sat in the middle with Luke on her lap. "Spin us around, would you?" she told Ethan. "But go slow."

Ethan stood at the edge of the play equipment, pushing gently against the metal bars. "What are you doing later?" he asked.

Now there was a memory.

Callie had met Ethan eleven years ago, across a study table at the Wichita State University library. They'd started talking about their college classes, and after an hour of whispering he'd said exactly the same thing.

What are you doing later?

Back then, she'd said "nothing" and their romance had begun. She'd met him after dinner at Augusta's Miller's Five drive-in, where they had ordered two root beer floats to go. They'd walked around downtown for over two hours, talking all the while. Augusta's downtown area had never been large, so they'd made the same loop several times.

Now Callie frowned as she whirled slowly around with Luke resting against her body. She wanted to say "nothing" again, just to hear Ethan's response, but in her confusion she didn't answer.

"Isabel said you were all planning to celebrate Luke's birthday together later this evening," Ethan said.

Oh. That was what he'd meant. What was she doing later tonight, *for Luke's birthday.*

"Nothing too exciting," she said. "I bought ingredients for a cake and a spaghetti dinner. He'll have his first big-boy meal followed by his first taste of chocolate cake."

"All those firsts sound fun."

"Luke had his first real haircut today, too," she said.

And he spent his first morning in the park with his daddy. He demanded his daddy's attention for the first time. And he played basketball with him.

However, neither father nor son would know today that they'd celebrated all those firsts together. They might never know.

All at once, dizziness overwhelmed Callie. "Stop pushing," she said. "I need to get off."

Ethan stopped the merry-go-round, and Callie sat for a minute, recovering. When Luke whimpered, she suspected that the motion had been lulling him to sleep.

"You think he wants to ride more?" Ethan asked. "I can sit with him now, if you'll push."

Callie smiled at her little boy. "No. See the pink under his eyes?"

"Sure."

"That means he's sleepy. I'd better take him to Josie's."

Ethan nodded. "All right. I really should head to Wichita. LeeAnn's been feeling neglected lately." He stared at Callie, as if he was surprised he'd said that to her.

Callie was glad that he had mentioned LeeAnn. If his girlfriend felt undervalued, maybe she'd find another cowboy who had more time for her. Then maybe she'd quit nagging Ethan about the divorce.

Then maybe he'd drop it.

"Unless you want to walk with me," Callie said. "If I put Luke in his stroller, we could walk him for a while and he'd probably go to sleep. It's such a nice day, we could park his stroller in the shade and enjoy the fresh air."

Ethan raised his eyebrows. "Really?"

What was she doing? Most definitely, her invitation had been a heart-driven impulse. But the gruff breathlessness in Ethan's response had caught her attention. He wanted to stay as much as she wanted him to.

In spite of LeeAnn. In spite of Callie's why nots.

Why shouldn't they take a walk together on the gorgeous May day that also happened to be their son's first birthday? Lots of divorcing couples must do the same.

Callie nodded. "Really."

As far as Luke was concerned, the plan worked like a charm. He was asleep within five minutes. Callie parked his stroller beneath a massive cottonwood tree and sat in the grass next to her husband, leaning against the tree trunk while they plucked tall dandelions.

A gentle breeze flowed through the branches overhead, the constant whir of the leaves inviting conversation. The rush of wind would carry their words away, keeping them private and safe.

They talked about Ethan's job and Callie's latest research. He loved the quick response time and the diversity of the helicopter patrol. She thought her current project might have a real impact on the treatment of ovarian cancer within the next decade.

Although they faced outward, toward the park road, Callie couldn't have been more aware of Ethan if she'd been eyeing him straight on. He had his long, jeans-clad legs stretched out and crossed at the ankles, next to hers.

She remembered their rock-solid feel, hot against her skin. Whenever he'd hugged her. Whenever they'd sat together in a car or on a sofa. In bed.

Wherever.

They discussed Isabel's house again, and Ethan's shirtsleeve tickled Callie's arm. After she'd brushed away the sensation for the third or fourth time, he leaned nearer. Now his arm rested heavily against hers.

Was he even aware that they were touching? Aware of the sensations he was provoking in her?

Callie considered moving away. But she treasured the solid weight of him so much that she remained. She recognized that this was just the sort of mindless attraction her mother had warned her about.

The conversation turned to Ethan's parents, who'd relocated to Arizona a year after Ethan and Callie were married. As long as the subject matter remained neutral, Callie felt comfortable talking to Ethan. A couple of times, she realized she was relaxing too much. She worried that she'd make some comment about Luke's day care experiences, or about some incredible thing he'd done back in Denver.

She managed well until Ethan sat up straighter to peer at Luke in his stroller. "Funny, he doesn't take after Isabel or her boyfriend. Sometimes when he concentrates, he reminds me a little bit of you." He chuckled. "Or even of me. He has hair similar to mine, doesn't he?"

"You think so?" Callie asked, her heart racing. "Well, that makes sense, I guess. Isabel has brown hair."

Ethan glanced at her. "Does Roger have brown eyes?"

He did, thank heaven. Dark brown eyes. Not warm amber ones. "Yes, he does," Callie said quickly.

Ethan returned his attention to the sleeping baby.

Callie worried that her little boy would wake up and grin at his new friend, and Ethan might realize where he'd seen similar eyes and dimples and hair before.

In the mirror this morning.

Panicking, Callie threw down the dandelions she'd been bunching into a bouquet and sprang to her feet. "I'd better get Luke home, after all," she said. "I still haven't made his cake or wrapped his gift from me. I'd be smart to use his nap time."

Ethan got up, too. "You won't wake him when you transfer him to the car seat?"

Callie was already starting to push the stroller toward the rental car. "I don't think so," she said. "All this fresh air has him pretty tuckered out."

"Do you need help?"

"No. You go on home. Call LeeAnn or do whatever. Have fun. Goodbye."

As she drove to Josie's apartment, Callie wondered

again if she had the wits to see this whole charade through. Every time she saw Ethan, she forgot most of her resolve. She'd be smart to avoid him.

She'd be smarter still to keep him away from Luke. A one-year-old might not communicate much, but Luke had been saying "momma" lately, pretty clearly. He also looked more and more like his daddy every day.

Now that Isabel's phone line was due for reconnection, avoiding Ethan might be easier. Callie would call before she took Luke by Isabel's house, she'd visit for only short spells and she'd keep the baby away whenever Ethan was expected.

Ethan didn't need to see her or Luke to help Isabel. Callie would instruct her sisters to put her estranged husband to work every time he showed up, even if they had to send him to the backyard with a bucket of cleaner and a scrub brush. The man was born to help. If Isabel asked him to, he'd probably scrape grime off the outside of the house.

Callie needed to remember three things: that Ethan had left her, that she alone had chosen to bring her precious boy into the world, and that she couldn't fathom losing her son entirely.

If Callie remembered those things, she'd find her resolve.

Chapter Seven

By the time Ethan had finished ripping out Isabel's ruined bathroom vanity, it was just after eight o'clock. Too late for him to make it to Wichita for the beginning of Lee-Ann's concert, or to launch another cleanup project here at the house. The city inspector was overworked, but Callie's middle sister was expecting her name to appear at the top of his waiting list at any moment. Then, she'd said, her new bathroom and kitchen cabinets would be installed.

Ethan was grateful for the break. His stiff hands and sore back reminded him that he wasn't some passionate kid out to save the world anymore. He heard Josie's radio playing in the second bedroom, so he went to check on her progress.

She'd knelt in the doorway to paint the very last corner of the room.

"Wouldn't this be Luke's room?" he asked.

Josie jumped, then chuckled as she glanced at him. "I forgot you were still here," she said. Squinting, she studied the room she'd been painting all evening. "Oh, yeah. Luke's room."

"Funny choice of color, for a baby's room," he said. "Is that tan or orange?"

"It's Majestic Gold. Very princely."

"Oh. Well, we got a lot done today," he said. "Guess it was a good idea to divide and conquer."

"Yes. We've really made progress."

"The old cabinets are in the basement and I fixed those bad spots on the walls," he said. "I'll just say goodbye to Izzy, then head home to Wichita."

"All right."

Ethan was more tired than he'd realized. The constant motions had kept his muscles fluid. Now they were stiff. And he was famished. He hadn't stopped for dinner, had he?

He should go. He could go hit an east-Wichita drive-through for a sandwich, and get home by nine. If he caught River's Bend's last set, he could buy LeeAnn a drink afterward. Although he'd talked to her this morning, had even treated her to breakfast at the Beacon, he knew she'd been jealous of the time he spent here in Augusta. He felt awful about it.

But at the moment the drive to Wichita appeared endless. A hamburger on the run didn't sound good, either. As far as Ethan knew, Callie's sisters hadn't eaten since he'd arrived early this afternoon.

"We never stopped for dinner," he said, causing Josie to chuckle again. "Aren't you hungry?"

"Sure." Josie maneuvered her legs around to sit cross-legged, then relaxed against the doorsill and looked up at him. "Callie was planning to bring something by, but she called a while ago and said Luke was fussing a lot. She decided to keep him at my apartment."

At the mention of Callie, Ethan felt a different kind of hunger. Foolish as it was, he'd missed seeing her today. Maybe he'd go by Josie's apartment to say hello, and also check on the little boy. "Is Luke okay?" he asked.

"Oh, sure. He's just teething. Callie would have given him a pain reliever, so he's probably asleep." Josie leaned forward and began to paint again.

He shouldn't go by. He might wake the baby. He should do the right thing, and spend time with LeeAnn.

"I noticed the pizza place is open for business again," he said. "Aren't you a mushroom fanatic?"

"Oh, my God! A thin pizza with mushrooms and green peppers sounds heavenly about now," Josie said, her eyes alight.

He chuckled. "The one in my heaven has Italian sausage, onions and a thick crust."

She gasped. Apparently, she wasn't picky about toppings.

"I could have a couple delivered," he offered, liking the idea more every second he thought about it.

Josie dipped her brush into the paint, slapped it against the rim of the can and painted gold over the last strip of primed wallboard.

He waited for her to tell him it was a bad idea. That she was too busy and that he should go home to order a pizza. Instead, she dropped the paintbrush and leaped up with a nimbleness that reminded him of their seven-year age difference. "I'm game," she said. "Let's go see what Izzy thinks."

They found Isabel in the kitchen, sweeping the floor where the cabinets used to be. From the back, she resembled Ella, but when she circled around to peer at Ethan and Josie, her expression was much more welcoming.

Ella had never taken to Ethan. Callie had avoided bringing him home for almost a year. When she had, Ella hadn't been pleased to hear that her oldest daughter was in love and planning to marry at nineteen.

After they were married, Ella had softened only slightly. Ethan didn't think Callie had ever told her mother that they were having trouble. She hadn't told her sisters, either, presumably until after he'd left. She'd wanted to make her own choices without her mother's influence, and she hadn't wanted her sisters to buy into Ella's thoughts about men. Even though she'd believed them herself.

"What are you two up to?" Isabel asked, smiling. "Did you do something tricky?"

"Nope," Josie said. "Ethan had an idea."

"Uh-oh." After leaning her broom against the wall, Isabel rested her hands on her hips. "Well, what is it?" she asked good-humoredly, as if she expected them to describe a prank of some kind.

"Pizza," Ethan said. "I want to buy you ladies a pizza, that's all."

No look of interest changed Isabel's tired expression. She glanced around her kitchen, and Ethan saw what she must be seeing. The tile hadn't been installed, the cabinets were gone and her table was quite obviously missing.

"Where would we eat?" she asked, sounding distressed. "My plates are packed in the attic."

That was right. Isabel loved to play hostess, didn't she? She wouldn't view his offer as a source of food. She'd worry about ensuring her guests' comfort. "We could have it delivered to Josie's place," Ethan said, shrugging.

"But Callie's there," Isabel said, blue eyes wide.

"I know." He chuckled.

Isabel gazed at Josie, her eyes narrowed. "She might not want pizza," she said in a precise tone.

Protecting Callie again. She must not know about that

sunny day at the park, when he and Callie had reclaimed
their friendship. "If she does, I'll share," Ethan said, ignoring another silent Blume battle. "She likes the same
kind I do. I don't see a problem."

"I feel bad about not feeding you," Isabel said.

"Don't. Pizza sounds good."

Isabel glared at Josie, who returned the look. They acted very much like the two teenagers to whom he'd once
offered secret driving lessons: tempted, but thinking hard
about the consequences should their mother find out.

They were making this a bigger decision than it needed to be. He'd only offered to buy them dinner.

"All right," Isabel said, apparently deciding that the reward was worth the risk. Whatever that was.

Minutes later, Ethan parked behind Josie's apartment
and realized he was the first to arrive. Good. He'd visit
with Callie privately while he had a chance. After they ate,
he'd have to race to Wichita to catch LeeAnn's last set.
He'd promised.

But as he walked toward the apartment, Josie drove up
in her truck, then Isabel in her car. Somehow, they managed to get into Josie's apartment before he did. Then they
closed the door behind them.

By the time he reached it, the door popped open to reveal all three Blume sisters standing in the entrance to Josie's living room.

Callie put an index finger to her lips and Isabel pointed one of hers at the baby, who was sleeping in a small,
portable crib near the sofa.

Josie motioned for him to follow her to the kitchen.
"You called the pizza place from your cell, right?" she
whispered. "How long till it arrives?"

"Forty minutes," he said in a normal voice.

"Shh!" Josie glared at him.

Callie entered the kitchen and sat at the table, then Isabel came in and opened the refrigerator. "Soda or beer?" she asked in a hushed voice as she peered inside.

It was soda for Callie and Isabel, beer for Josie and himself. Josie sat at the table across from Callie, and Isabel leaned against the counter next to him. The hiss and snap of the four drinks opening sounded loud. All three women paused, drinks in hand, and listened for a moment.

When the apartment remained quiet, they smirked at one another and sipped their drinks without speaking.

Maybe Luke was a very light sleeper.

The room felt small.

And hot.

Ethan was too grimy and tired to stand around drinking beer and whispering for forty minutes.

Maybe he should have gone home.

"Want to shower while you're waiting?" Josie whispered, pointing toward his chest.

Ethan glanced down. He had dry wall dust everywhere. He even felt silt between his teeth. "I'm fine," he lied.

Isabel pulled a fragment of insulation off his shirtsleeve. "Oh, please, make yourself comfortable," she said. "I'll feel awful if you don't. Forty minutes is just long enough for you to get clean and for me to run your clothes through the washing machine."

Fifteen minutes later, Ethan had showered and dressed in a pair of gray sweat shorts and a big robe that Josie had found among her things. The clothes fit Ethan well, so he suspected that they belonged to one of her guy friends. It was none of his business, but he was glad that at least one of the Blume sisters had a healthy attitude toward men.

After tiptoeing past the sleeping baby, he discovered the kitchen empty. He grabbed his beer and located the Blume girls sitting on the floor of Josie's balcony, talking politics.

Callie's mother might have had some social fears, but she'd raised three savvy daughters. Ethan had always gotten a kick out of the family's prolonged debates that could run from religion to rhubarb and back again in minutes. He claimed a spot between Callie and the sliding door and joined right in.

When they heard the pizza delivery truck drive up and park, he met the guy at the door to pay, grabbed everyone another drink and rejoined them.

Before he knew it, the pizzas were gone and they'd talked until eleven-thirty. He'd had five beers to Josie's three, and he'd blown LeeAnn off entirely. He had no doubt that he'd find two or three messages from her on his answering machine.

Damn it all, anyway.

He mentioned leaving, and that's when Isabel realized that she had forgotten to transfer his clothes from the washer to the dryer.

Ethan studied his unusual attire. No shirt, a robe, shorts, bare legs and bare feet. "Oh well, what are the chances of anyone seeing me between here and home?"

"Oh, Ethan!" Isabel exclaimed.

"I'll be fine," he said. "Just help me find my shoes."

"I put those in the washer, too," Isabel said. When everyone stared at her, she shrugged. "They were *full* of dust and insulation."

"I can wear them wet."

"I'd feel terrible," Isabel said. "I must be getting worn-out. I've been an awful hostess."

"You're not a hostess," Ethan said. "You're the friend and sister we're all helping. Relax."

"You've had a few beers, Eth," she argued.

"I know. I'm fine."

All three women looked skeptical.

He was fine!

He was a police officer. He knew when fine was fine.

But when you grew up in a house where alcohol and boys were forbidden, you might wonder how many beers a man could drink and be all right.

"Aw, heck, Eth. Why don't you just stay tonight?" Josie said. "Guys crash in my recliner all the time. I'll get you a pillow and some blankets to make it extra comfy."

Isabel frowned at her, then at him again, then at Callie. She *kept* staring at Callie.

Apparently, Callie would decide.

Apparently, he had little say in the matter.

"Okay," Callie said. "But I'll have to sleep in here on the sofa," she said.

Isabel colored. "Oh! Well, of course. I didn't—"

"I insist," Callie interjected. "I know you're protective of your baby, but I'll take good care of him."

"Uh-huh."

"Ethan and I are *married,*" Callie argued, even though Isabel had just agreed. "You and Josie should have privacy."

"All right. Good plan," Isabel said, sounding uncertain.

It was a good plan, except that Ethan was sleeping in the same room as Callie and a baby who slept a lot more soundly than his mother and aunts believed.

The Blume sisters took turns showering. Within minutes, Callie entered the living room wearing sleep pants and a tank top. With wet hair and a freshly scrubbed face, she bore an air of sweet vulnerability. She fussed with the items in her luggage for a few minutes, then she eased on-to the sofa and pulled the covers to her chin.

Ethan lay on the recliner, flat on his back with eyes wide-open. Suddenly, he wasn't at all tired.

Callie flipped onto her tummy; he flopped over onto his side. She adjusted her pillow, fluffing and punching it; he bent his knees, fitting them into a tight spot. She scratched a spot on her shoulder, sighing; he yanked the blankets over his feet, sighing.

He flipped over.

So did she.

"Can't sleep?" he muttered.

"Nope."

He hesitated for only a moment, then said, "Follow me."

He got up, grabbed his blankets and walked out the sliding glass door, waiting until Callie had followed him before he shut it behind them.

They sat side by side, each with a blanket over their shoulders, and didn't speak for a long while.

THE COOL, STILL NIGHT made Callie appreciate Ethan's thoughtfulness in bringing the blankets. From Josie's second-floor balcony, much of the sky was visible—it was a deep, velvet blue. The magical night made it hard to be-lieve that less than two months ago, heavy rains had caused life-changing disruption to so many people in this town.

Seemingly, it had caused a similar disruption to Callie's life. Things would surely return to normal when she went back to Denver, but at this moment she felt changed.

She wondered if she'd be able to cope with the distance between her and her sisters again, and if her new memo-ries of Ethan would make coping that much more difficult.

It was also hard to believe that just one week after she'd decided she shouldn't sit next to Ethan in the fresh air, talking about things—shouldn't, in fact, allow him to be around her or Luke at all—here she was, sitting next to Ethan in the fresh *night* air, not talking about anything.

With Luke in the very next room.

At least the baby was asleep.

With Luke's eyes and mouth closed, Ethan would have to get right down next to him to see a resemblance.

Ethan nudged Callie with his shoulder. "The stars are out," he said, pointing to a trio of lights low in the western sky.

Not stars. Planets.

And a good idea, to use her aptitude for science to analyze the romance out of a volatile situation. "Those are planets," she said. "Mercury's the one dipping into the horizon and Mars is the orange one. The third one is Saturn, I believe."

He didn't say anything, so she pulled the covers higher on her chest and fell silent.

"Callie?"

His soft bidding sounded dangerous. She ignored him.

"Cal, look at me."

Okay. No way to ignore that. She glanced at him and regretted it instantly. He was staring at her mouth. His expression suggested passion, and Callie felt a wild pang of yearning before she turned away.

Her ploy to keep things factual hadn't worked, and her body had gone haywire. Her shirt chafed against her breasts, her lower limbs trembled and her mouth pouted, as if revealing its readiness for a kiss.

Kisses.

"You don't have to impress me," he said, his voice husky. "I know you're a smart woman. Relax."

"I am relaxed," she said, ignoring her mutinous body as she reminded herself of three things. She was talking to her estranged husband. Who was the unwitting father of her precious child. Whom she couldn't lose.

"Your mother did that, too," Ethan said.

"Did what?"

"Shrouded her feelings behind debate. Whenever she was really nervous about something, she'd bring up the latest political controversy."

Had she done that? Callie had always considered her mother a pure intellectual who cared only about her kids and knowledge. Not feelings. "You think so?"

"Oh, yeah."

Callie didn't doubt it. Ethan might have missed a few cues in this situation, understandably, but he was normally good at reading people.

"Mom had it rough," Callie said. "She lost her parents when she was sixteen, then she married too young. When Dad left, she had three kids to raise. She had to be lonely."

"Probably."

"I have vague memories of Dad," Callie said, thinking of the tall, quiet man who had once taken her to hear calliope music, played by a mechanical clown at a Wichita amusement park. "Before he left, she was always upset with him. Later, she directed her anger toward all men."

"You knew that about her?" Ethan asked.

"Sure," Callie said. "I think I saw her for who she was. A very smart, very stubborn woman who could have used a good friend. If she had lived longer, my sisters and I might have grown into the role."

Ethan sighed, then shifted so that their arms were touching. The contact felt as good as it had the other day in the park.

"After she died, you isolated yourself just as she had," Ethan said quietly. "I wanted to be there for you, but you wouldn't let me help."

Callie was horrified. She had always valued Ethan's opinion. She'd listened to him, hadn't she?

But back then, they'd argued a lot. She'd said spiteful things during those clashes. She remembered telling Ethan once that he rarely knew what he was talking about. She'd implied that he was weak-minded, and that she'd be better off without him.

That had never been true, but she'd said it. Callie's mother had always said the same things about her father. It had likely not been true in that case, either.

Ethan maneuvered away from her, making her miss his warmth, then he grasped her chin and pulled her face toward his. "I knew you were struggling," he said softly. "Don't worry too much. We both made mistakes."

She gazed at him for only a minute. Even in the darkness, she could feel his sincerity. She was grateful for it.

Grateful, also, that she hadn't become some bitter, hardened woman. Luke must have softened her.

And perhaps she was different because she'd once had Ethan's very devoted love. She might have failed at marriage, but she recognized that men could be strong allies. She could never become exactly like her mother.

"You've always been as smart as Ella, and as stubborn," he said. "But you allow yourself to feel. Maybe it helped to have sisters."

"And you," she admitted. "It helped that I had you."

This time, she held his stare. She should have told him that years ago. Callie knew she'd always remember this moment. She saw the kiss coming, and she had no inclination to fight it.

Not right now. The reasons for this particular kiss, from both sides, were very pure.

His hot, pliant lips tasted of the same toothpaste she'd used a while ago. She opened her mouth and let him know that she was still soft. Still okay. That the past two years hadn't hardened her.

The kiss changed quickly, from curious to sensual. When Ethan slid his hands beneath her blanket to caress her breasts through her pajama top, she shivered.

Well, some things might have changed. Her body had. She wondered if he noticed. Wondered how much childbirth had changed her in other ways.

And wished she could ask him.

He growled.

She smiled, but lost that smile immediately when he put both hands on her waist and pulled her around, lifting her to sit across his lap. "Sweet mercy, you feel good," he said, caressing her hips as he adjusted her body to fit against his arousal.

This would be the appropriate time to stop. She could say she'd heard a noise, then run inside to check on Luke.

She didn't want to. She wanted to kiss Ethan. She wanted to feel his hands on her needful places and she wanted to relive the deep security of his affection.

"You do, too," she said quietly.

He tugged his blanket around her shoulders, enclosing them in a private world on Josie's balcony. Callie slipped her hands beneath the opening to his robe, relishing the feel of his warm, muscular chest.

He hadn't changed at all, thank heaven.

She wrapped her hands behind his shoulders and slid

nearer. When he kissed her again, she closed her eyes, even against the darkness. This would be okay, she thought wildly, if she couldn't see.

If she didn't think about why nots.

Running a line of kisses along his collarbone, she pressed a hot, open kiss against his neck while he slid his hands beneath her shirt, exploring her changed breasts with erotic interest.

Luke began to fuss.

Callie ignored those first weak mewlings, hoping sleep would win out. She kissed along Ethan's jaw, traveling toward his mouth. Wishing he'd touch her nipples again. Wishing he'd kiss them.

Wishing.

Luke began to cry in earnest.

Ethan removed his hands.

She stopped kissing.

Damn.

The baby had fallen to sleep early after she'd given him the medicine. She'd expected him to wake up tonight with a wet diaper or a hungry belly or both.

Just not now.

Callie opened her eyes to Ethan's gaze. "Guess that's my cue to leave," she said.

"Isabel won't tend to him?"

Isabel. That was right, she'd let Ethan believe that idiotic story about her sister being Luke's mother. It was so easy to forget.

Callie wished she had told Ethan the truth. She wanted to blurt it out right now.

She could take him by the hand and lead him inside to Luke. She'd tell him to study the boy, and then she'd spill the entire story in Josie's living room.

But she feared his response. If he reacted in anger and took legal action against her, she couldn't fathom a future without either her husband or her son.

Perhaps Luke's crying had been lucky in its timing.

"Isabel won't awaken this quickly," Callie said. "She's pretty exhausted. If I get to Luke before she does, she can sleep. I'd better go inside."

"Wait."

Her spot on Ethan's lap had felt delectable a minute ago. Now it embarrassed her. She wanted to scramble off of him. Go to her baby.

Escape to her lonely life.

Ethan tugged at her top, smoothing it over her breasts and belly. As he brushed a strand of hair behind her ear, he said, "I thought you might want to be presentable in case one of your sisters comes into the living room to check on Luke, too."

Callie didn't stir, thinking it might be best to ignore the too-intimate contact of their bodies. "Okay," she said. "You know I won't come back out here tonight, right?"

He didn't move, either.

Callie held his gaze, hoping to make her silent communication clear.

This was a mistake. We can't try again in a half hour. Please don't make this demand on me again, and if I start something with you, ignore me.

"Right," he said. "I'll sneak in after I hear that Luke has quieted."

"You're not coming in now?" she asked.

"No. It'd be best for me to wait a few minutes," he said. He settled his hands on her hips, pressing her downward to communicate *his* unspoken meaning.

He was still hard. Ready.

Of course. He wouldn't be able to jump up and tend to a baby, turning off his desire as if it were a light switch. And yet he'd been considerate of her.

He was such a good man.

Callie might feel some small regret about getting physically involved with Ethan tonight, but stopping was worse. Mostly, she regretted not letting Ethan know that the crying baby was his.

He'd come inside anyway, if he knew.

She wondered what else he would do. Would he react in anger, in joy or in some combination that would complicate their lives forever? If she knew that, she'd know how to talk to him.

"All right." Callie put a hand on Ethan's shoulder and stood up, disentangling legs and blankets and emotions on the way. Then she stepped past Ethan and reentered Josie's living room to tend to her baby.

Chapter Eight

The baby was crying again. Ethan opened his eyes just in time to watch Callie roll off the couch and peer into the crib, then pat the little guy on his bottom. "Lukey, what's the matter?" she whispered. "Are you hungry?"

The baby quieted. Callie smiled and picked him up, cuddling him against her while she padded to the kitchen. She returned with a bottle, then sat on the sofa with Luke to begin feeding him.

When she glanced toward the recliner, Ethan closed his eyes and pretended to be asleep. He kept thinking if he knew Callie's thoughts, he'd know the answer to so many riddles. Why she'd lost faith in them as a couple, for one thing. He might have left her physically, but she'd been the instigator.

He might also discover why she was resisting the divorce. She might put minor things off, but when it came to important issues, she generally took charge. Her hot-cold behavior didn't make sense.

Or maybe it did. Maybe she was as mixed-up about their attraction as he was.

When he'd come inside last night, she'd been holding Luke, humming to him with her eyes shut. Ethan had remade his temporary bed on the recliner and within minutes Callie had put the baby in the crib, returned to the sofa and gone to sleep.

As if their private patio party had been a dream.

It was hard not to smile at the robust sounds of the baby's drinking. Ethan peeked, noting the way the boy's stout little hands latched onto the bottle.

Callie's attachment to the boy was understandable.

He couldn't imagine her handing the baby back to Isabel and heading for Denver. Saddened at that thought, Ethan squeezed his eyes closed again. Callie might be independent, but she needed people more than she acknowledged.

When Ethan heard voices coming from the bedroom, he realized that Callie's sisters were awake, too. He should get moving. He sat up, noticing Callie's tangled hair and the slight puffiness around her eyes that made her appear sleepy.

And sexy.

He wondered if she had slept, or if last night had upset her too much.

"Morning," he said.

She glanced up and gave a slight nod.

Luke also spied Ethan, and grinned widely, with his teeth gripping the bottle's nipple. Then he adjusted his fingers on the bottle, returned to his drinking and watched Callie again.

He was a really great kid.

Both Callie and the baby smiled at each other, ignoring him. "Is Luke okay?" Ethan asked, remembering that he'd been teething yesterday.

Callie leveled a gaze at him, her expression cool. "He's fine. Just hungry."

"What about you? Are you all right?"

"Why wouldn't I be?"

So Ethan knew, then, what to expect from Callie today. Composure.

He'd thought she might laugh about last night, saying something about reliving old feelings. Or she might have been hyperserious, trying to understand why they'd slipped and whether it had meant anything.

Either response would have acknowledged this attraction between them. Perhaps even a new caring.

But she'd closed herself off again. She was handling this in the same manner she'd handled her thoughts about the marriage—by pretending it had never happened.

He might have known.

The thing to do, he decided, was simply to follow her lead. He didn't want to embarrass her in front of her sisters, and he was adult enough to know that even the strongest physical attraction to a person didn't have to mean more than what it was.

He'd wanted her. She'd wanted him.

They were admitting only that.

After pressing the lever on the side of the recliner, Ethan slid off the chair and folded his blanket, stacking it on the arm. Funny, Josie had given him two. He must have left the brown one on the patio. He thought about searching for it, but when he glanced up, he caught Callie staring at his bare chest and almost-bare backside.

He still had on Josie's gray shorts, and he'd left the robe draped over the arm of the recliner.

Callie must have seen him completely naked a few thousand times, and this wasn't the first time her attention had had an impact. He averted his gaze, remembering how quickly she aroused him.

"We'd better get you some clothes," she said, stepping across the room to hand the baby to him. "Take Luke for a minute. I'll go check the dryer."

Sometime in the night, Ethan's clothes had tumbled dry. They were wrinkled but wearable. He dressed in the bathroom, then met Callie's sisters in the kitchen, where they were sitting around Josie's small table sipping drinks, nibbling on doughnuts and talking about their plans for the day.

Isabel motioned for him to help himself to coffee, and Josie nudged the box of doughnuts toward him. Neither paused in their conversation at all, yet Ethan was comforted by their casual acceptance of his presence.

He'd just taken a bite of a chocolate long john when Callie walked past him, Luke on her hip, and sat in the third chair to join in the discussion about today's plans for furniture shopping.

She was making it quite clear, at least to him, that he should leave. He no longer fit in this kitchen with her family.

Not today.

He finished the doughnut in five bites, downed the coffee and carried his cup to the sink to rinse it and stack it in the dishwasher.

No matter what Callie thought, he fit. He'd known these girls since Josie was young enough to have scabs on her knees from falling off her bicycle. He was fairly certain he'd been Isabel's first crush.

He fit.

Moments later, Callie's sisters walked him to the door, thanking him for the pizza, reverting to the polite behavior that a person might lavish on company.

He responded as a gracious guest, but he'd preferred things the other way.

As he drove home, Ethan's mind was full of Callie and last night. He realized that he should keep following her lead and ignore what had happened on that balcony. He should pass it off as a momentary slip and get on with his new life.

When he saw LeeAnn sitting in her car outside his house, however, Ethan admitted to himself that his new life wasn't always a barrel of laughs. He hadn't forgotten Lee-Ann this time. Not really. He'd simply chosen to stay in Augusta, knowing that he'd have to explain his actions to her later.

Now was that time.

He drove past her into his garage, then slid out of his car to wait for her. When she walked in behind him, he didn't even bother trying to smile. LeeAnn must be as tired of his excuses as he was.

"Hi, stranger." She grinned feebly at him. When her eyes fell to his wrinkled shirt, her smile disappeared.

He wore the same shirt he'd worn to the Beacon for breakfast yesterday. "I can explain," he said. "But let's at least go inside."

She followed him through to his living room, and at his prompting sat on the sofa.

Ethan glanced at the mail on the floor near the door, at the closed drapes and at the blinking answering machine light. That'd be LeeAnn's message, he was certain.

He wished he had a few moments alone at home, to read through his mail and open his drapes and think about what he was doing.

But LeeAnn was here, waiting. How could he convince himself that she was the girl for him and Callie wasn't, when he hopped straight from one set of expectations to the next?

He sat beside her and took her hands. "LeeAnn, don't worry. We're fine," he said, and paused to think.

Maybe he should simply tell LeeAnn that it was over. That he'd been thinking too much about his wife, and that his relationship with LeeAnn had fallen victim to bad timing.

But he wasn't sure.

Callie had dismissed him. She might be physically attracted to him, but her opinions of their relationship status hadn't changed. As far as he knew, she intended to return to Denver when her sister moved back into her house.

As far as he knew, he hadn't been invited to return to Denver with Callie. He'd screwed that up when he'd left.

LeeAnn was exciting, pretty and available. She most certainly didn't ignore him. If he'd never met Callie, he might be head over heels in love with LeeAnn or some other woman who'd caught his eye.

Maybe *he* was the victim of bad timing.

He should remember that he was going on with things. Divorcing Callie. Marching forward with a new woman who was ready for a relationship.

He could do that.

When LeeAnn raised her eyebrows to prompt the discussion, Ethan noticed the pinks and purples she'd painted on her eyelids today. Her lips were crimson. She hadn't worn her cowboy hat this morning, so her black hair lay in loose curls around her shoulders.

Today, all her frippery looked like armor. He wouldn't blame her if she pulled out a sword.

"We're fine," he repeated, feeling this time as if it were true. "You knew I went to Augusta to help Isabel."

"Right. To rip out some old cabinets," LeeAnn said. "I remember."

He shrugged. "I stayed too late, that's all. By the time

I finished, it was almost nine o'clock and none of us had eaten lunch or dinner."

"Poor thing."

"I ordered pizza for everyone."

She nodded. "And it took *all night* to eat it," she said, her expression doubtful.

And he'd gotten physically involved with Callie. He'd gone beyond kisses to touches. If the baby hadn't cried, he would have made love to his wife.

LeeAnn didn't deserve this treatment. No woman did.

Ethan shoved a hand through his hair. "Listen, I'll admit I'm confused, but I didn't stay overnight so I could spend the time with Callie. I had some beer, and Callie's sister was afraid that I shouldn't drive home."

LeeAnn's eyes widened. "How much did you drink?"

"Not that much. A few. It's hard to explain, but those girls grew up in a house where any drinking was considered sinful. I think their dad might have been an alcoholic. Isabel would worry about one beer."

"She's backward?"

Ethan felt a bristle of defensiveness.

"No, she's not. Just sheltered."

LeeAnn must have heard the strain in his voice. "Okay."

"I'd already missed your second set, so I chose to stay."

"Okay," LeeAnn repeated.

"I slept alone on a recliner in Josie's living room."

For the first time today, LeeAnn smiled a real smile. She'd been worried about his sleeping arrangements, that was all. And his sleeping arrangements were the very thing that had caused him turmoil. LeeAnn was a sharp woman.

Ethan relaxed, too. "If it makes you feel better, I have a crick in my neck."

She kept smiling, then motioned for him to turn around on the sofa. She smoothed her palms against his neck and shoulders. "Our second set went long," she said in a voice that sounded musical now. "I came home and crashed, but when I never heard from you, I did worry. Just ignore my answering machine messages."

"All right."

Normally, he liked LeeAnn's firm touch against his shoulders. Now he was ready for her to go. Ethan pulled her hands away. "That's enough."

"It isn't helping?" she asked.

"I'm just tired."

And he craved a day of privacy.

"So, what are you doing today?" she asked, still sitting behind him. She wrapped her arms around his chest.

He should make something up. That he had to work today, or that he'd promised to help someone with something, or that he was over a month late paying his taxes.

But he didn't want to lie. He hated lying.

He just made damn excuses all the time.

"Nothing," he said. "No plans."

LeeAnn lifted her hands to his shoulders again, swiveling him around. Then she smiled brightly. "Want to come over?" she asked. "We could visit my folks. If you bring your swimsuit, we could use their pool."

Swimming sounded great. Visiting LeeAnn's parents didn't. Nice as they were, he didn't want to talk to them today. Or to anyone, really.

He didn't want to try to fit into a family that wasn't his. No matter how much a person loved their in-laws, when the marriage ended, they were often left wondering what had happened to that connection.

No way he was going to explain all that to LeeAnn. This

date could be his penance for neglecting her. "Swimming sounds great," he said.

"Good. We're on. What are you doing Wednesday night?" she asked. "I thought we could have dinner together."

Okay. LeeAnn deserved a night out, too. It'd be fun to dress up and hit the town. "All right."

"I know you work next weekend, but the Saturday after that you'll come to hear River's Bend, right? Our new songs sound really good."

LeeAnn was pushing his guilt buttons, wasn't she? "I'd enjoy coming to hear you," he said.

"And we can go out later," she added. "It's been a long time since we've gone dancing."

It had. And Ethan could handle that, too. However, he needed to get control of his guilt before he promised away the next six months of his life. He stood up. "I've got some things to do this morning. Why don't you go home and relax? I'll pick you up in a couple of hours. Say, about noon?"

LeeAnn lifted her eyebrows. "It's eleven-thirty, now."

Damn.

CALLIE CARRIED Luke into Isabel's house and discovered a small crowd. Her sister had arranged trays of store-bought cookies and iced raspberry tea on her new countertops, and she'd invited friends to come see the recently finished kitchen.

Roger stood talking to Isabel near the sink. His shoulders were slumped and faint circles ringed his eyes. With his car keys dangling from one hand, he appeared ready to leave. He must be taking a break from his farm chores. His kids sat on the pristine tile next to the back door, crunching away at a small mountain of cookies.

Three of Josie's friends had congregated with her over by the new refrigerator. They'd declined the sweet and simple fare, choosing instead to celebrate with beer.

Except for the church volunteers, the contractors and one other notable exception, everyone who'd played a big part in helping Isabel was here.

But then, Ethan couldn't be here with Josie's buddies, Roger and the kids. They all knew Luke belonged to Callie.

Thank heaven Josie had been on her toes a couple of weeks ago, when Ethan had arrived to help in the basement. She'd kept him from going inside to talk to the gang. Despite her mixed feelings, she'd covered for her big sister. Again.

And they'd all managed to invite Ethan only on days when he'd be alone with the Blumes. Keeping the secret had become as much a chore as any of the flood cleanup.

Before she returned to Denver, Callie would take her sisters out for a nice dinner. She owed them at least that.

The kitchen looked great, or at least what Callie could see of it did. White laminate cabinets and ceramic floor tiles were affordable choices, yet they made the small kitchen appear elegant. The room still had a gaping hole where the new range would be placed, but it was otherwise finished.

After Callie had walked in and greeted everyone, Josie and her gang circled her to comment on Luke's Kansas City Royals baseball outfit, part of Josie's birthday gift to him. Josie's friend Gabriel commented on the boy's superb taste in ball clubs, then Josie took the baby and invited her friends to join her in the front yard, so she could push Luke on a new plastic baby swing.

Callie crossed to Isabel and Roger. "What do you two think of the kitchen?" she asked, smiling.

Roger's daughter shouted, catching his attention. He frowned toward his kids and didn't answer.

"I love the countertops," Isabel said. "I think I'm going to have fun in here."

"I do, too," Callie said.

A movement by the door sent both Isabel and Roger across the kitchen to stop a full-blown cookie-throwing battle. Once the kids were subdued, Roger said goodbye and the four of them headed out the door.

When she found herself alone, Callie munched on a chocolate chip cookie and scrutinized the room again. The entire house had taken shape. Isabel needed to add shelves and finish the walls downstairs, then she'd get the city inspector here to approve the last phases of work. She needed to replace the range and more of the ruined furnishings, but she'd be able to move home very soon.

She could return to her normal life.

Callie didn't know if she would recognize hers. She'd been in Kansas long enough to feel at home here again. Eight years ago, she had left with Ethan after she'd been accepted into the University of Colorado's graduate biochemistry program. Ethan had found work with Denver's police squad. She'd been so excited.

She could hardly remember the big allure. She loved her job, certainly. Her co-workers' appreciation still surprised her, sometimes. Her townhome was beautiful and Luke thrived under the care of BioLab's excellent day care staff.

But Callie didn't get into the Colorado lifestyle as much as others did. Despite her co-workers, some nice neighbors and her son, Denver was lonely without Ethan.

That didn't matter.

Her research at BioLabs was important. Her lab had

been awarded a grant to develop a new drug that would aid in the early detection and treatment of certain forms of ovarian cancer. She couldn't give that up. In any case, moving here wasn't an option. Ethan would be too close.

As it was, she'd have to think of an explanation for Isabel to use if Ethan visited her after Callie left with Luke. She hadn't thought of a thing. All she knew was that she needed to be gone. That her heart was certain to break again. And that Ethan would have made a terrific father.

Isabel returned from walking Roger and the kids to his truck, then reclaimed her spot next to Callie.

"Time for them to go, huh?" Callie asked.

"Mmm-hmm. Roger just brought them by to admire the kitchen. He's taking them to their mother's."

"At least you didn't get stuck with them."

Isabel shrugged. "Actually, I'd prefer to keep them around. Taking care of them is a nice break for me."

Callie nodded. Sometimes, Isabel acted as if she cared as much for the kids as the dad. Or more.

"Oh! I meant to show you something," Isabel said, crossing toward her basement steps. "Hang on."

A moment later, she appeared around the corner carrying a green metal toolbox. "Isn't this Ethan's?" she asked.

It looked familiar, but a lot of men must own similar boxes. Callie pursed her lips. "Where did you find it?"

"Behind the old kitchen cabinets, downstairs."

"Then it's probably his. Ask him next time you see him."

"He hasn't been by for a while," Isabel said.

Callie knew. Lord, she knew. She'd kept telling herself she was glad she hadn't seen Ethan for a week. That his absence was exactly what she'd wanted.

The fact that she'd missed him wasn't the point. She'd

studied Pavlov. Her interactions with Ethan might have en-couraged a hunger for him, but eventually she'd stop crav-ing something she wasn't rewarded for.

Surely.

"Well, he'll come soon," Isabel said. "He shows up most Saturdays, doesn't he? Maybe tomorrow, he'll call. I could use help assembling those metal shelves."

And Callie would stay away.

"Maybe."

But Saturday came and went, and Ethan didn't call or come by. The toolbox sat on the floor next to Isabel's front door. Every time Luke came near it, he'd stop to sit by it and toy with the locks, bang on the lid or drop his pacifier on top.

Callie grew tired of seeing the infernal thing, which brought up too many questions.

Would he come? When? What would happen?

On Wednesday, Callie asked Josie to take the toolbox to Wichita with her when she went to work. Josie refused. She claimed that returning Ethan's property wasn't her re-sponsibility. She told Callie that she should take it to him, and also initiate a discussion about the genealogy of an adorable one-year-old boy.

Callie didn't have the heart to ask Isabel to take it by. The woman was working nonstop, still finishing house de-tails while trying to restart some of her craft work at Jo-sie's apartment in the evenings.

So the toolbox had remained just inside Isabel's front door, reminding Callie of how much she wanted to see the man she didn't want to see.

On the next Saturday, after it had become clear that Eth-an wasn't going to show up again, Callie went to Isabel's to help. She busied herself helping her sister put clean dishes into cabinets while Luke napped in Isabel's quiet, newly furnished bedroom.

"I thought I'd take that toolbox to Ethan this evening," Callie said.

Isabel's head emerged from behind a crate of pots and pans. "Really?"

"I'd be gone only a short while," Callie said as she dropped a handful of forks into the drawer. "We're almost finished here, and I don't know if he'll make it back to Augusta before I go home."

"Well, good," Isabel said.

"I won't be telling him about Luke, though. In fact, I hoped you might babysit. Still want that break from clean-up chores?"

"You bet." Isabel placed their mother's iron skillet in a low cabinet. "I'll have a blast with Luke. He usually goes to sleep around eight-thirty, right? And doesn't he wake up around three in the morning, sometimes?"

Callie sighed as she transferred spoons from a box to the drawer. "I'll certainly be home by three."

Isabel had disappeared behind the door again. "I'm not saying you won't. But if Luke wakes up and you're not here, I'll check his diaper or feed him. I'm telling you not to worry. That's all."

Stopping her work, Callie stared at the cabinet door until Isabel glanced around it again. "I won't worry. But I'll be gone long enough to get there, give the box to Ethan and drive back," she said.

"I'm sure." Isabel batted her eyelashes.

Callie should never have told her sisters about that patio escapade. She'd told them only to explain about the blanket Ethan had left outside. She hadn't given many details. Only that things had gone too far.

She certainly wasn't heading to Wichita for another make-out session, no matter what Isabel believed.

Moments later, Callie dialed Ethan's number using Josie's cell phone, while Josie worked nearby in the basement, humming the tune to an old, sexually suggestive rock song.

"Shh!" Callie hissed as Ethan's phone rang. "Just keep scrubbing."

"Hi, Ethan, it's me," she said, cringing when Josie broke into verse.

"'Lo, Callie." Ethan sounded surprised.

Josie sang louder, so Callie strode up the steps and out to the front porch. "I'm calling to ask what you're doing tonight." As soon as the words left her mouth, she regretted her phrasing. Josie's teasing had flustered her.

"Doing?"

"I think you left your toolbox at Isabel's," she explained. "I want to bring it by."

He hesitated for a minute, then said, "I guess I did leave it. I hadn't missed it yet."

"May I bring it by?"

"You don't need to. I'll pick it up."

"Tonight?"

"I have plans tonight, but I could come to Augusta tomorrow afternoon, maybe, or next week."

And she'd have to worry about the whole Luke problem, and she'd go slowly insane from seeing the dang thing sitting next to Isabel's front door.

"No. I'll bring it," she said. "I can get to your house and leave again before you go out."

"Okay. Come any time before eight."

Callie drove to west Wichita two hours later, and wasn't surprised to discover that Ethan lived in a family neigh-

borhood. Down the street, a group of boys played basketball in a driveway. At the house next to his, two young girls
skipped rope.

A typical bachelor might not choose this neighborhood,
but Ethan would. No doubt he called the basketball play-
ers and little girls by their first names. That gregariousness
had made Ethan perfect for her, once upon a time.

As she walked to the door, Callie became more and
more nervous. It didn't help that those infernal song lyr-
ics kept replaying in her mind.

Tonight was the night for the return of a toolbox, dang
it. That was all.

She rang the doorbell, then held the toolbox in front of
her, as if to protect herself from the impact of seeing him
again.

The ploy failed. He was stunning. He'd dressed in a
black button-down shirt and khaki pants that looked sexy
on his long legs. Immediately, he took the toolbox and put
it down just inside his front door.

"What? No baby?" he asked, dimples flashing. "I can
hardly remember seeing you without the little guy."

Callie nearly panicked at his question, and she was
glad she'd come alone, tonight. The mixed-up aunt-
mother story would be more plausible this way. "No. He's
at home with Isabel," she said.

He stepped backward. "Want to come in for a moment?"

Callie peered at him. She should go, especially since
he'd already taken the toolbox. But she was curious about
his house. Curious about what he'd been doing. "You
have time?"

He shrugged. "It's only seven-twenty."

He entered his living room, and she followed him. The

oversize furniture didn't surprise her, but the tidiness did. Ethan wasn't a slob, but he usually had at least four projects going at once. Their apartment had always been messy with belongings—a basketball from his afternoon game, a hammer from helping a co-worker fix a roof leak.

She'd complained then, but now she recognized that his clutter had been a good kind, indicative of his busy life.

"Nice place," she said.

He motioned toward his sofa. "Have a seat."

Callie sat, thinking of the items that filled her house in Denver these days. She'd traded the hammer for a baby gym and the basketball for stuffed toys.

She'd traded the man for a baby boy.

The thought upset her.

"How is Isabel's house coming along?" Ethan asked as he sat adjacent to her, on one of a pair of plump, chocolate-brown chairs.

"She's almost ready to return to the house."

"That's great."

"I know."

Neither said it. But Ethan held her gaze, as if to acknowledge that she'd return to Denver soon.

They'd be over. Again.

Thank heaven he didn't mention the divorce.

Maybe things had cooled off with LeeAnn, making the divorce more formality than necessity. "Well, I'd better go," she said. "You're going out."

Her last statement hung in the air between them. It had been an invitation for him to reveal where he was going, and with whom.

"It's still early," he said. "You want something to drink before you make the drive?"

If she stayed, she might learn more about the state of

his relationship with LeeAnn. Callie smiled an encouragement.

"How's lemonade sound?" he asked.

"Mmm."

He got up, then stood gazing at her. "Come to the kitchen with me?"

Seizing the chance to see more of his house, she followed him through to a large kitchen with two skylights and a table full of clutter. Here was the basketball, the box of candy some neighborhood kid must have sold him and about a week's worth of newspapers.

Callie grinned at the sight, then walked over to stand next to Ethan at the counter, watching him put lemons in his juicer to squeeze them. He poured the juice into two tall glasses, added water, sugar and cracked ice. Finally, he handed her a glass and leaned against the counter next to her to drink his.

He probably ate his meals right here in the very same spot. The thought comforted her. He'd adjusted to life without her, but not entirely.

As Callie sipped her drink, she noticed some items on the opposite counter—car keys, a wallet…and a florist's box.

So the romance with LeeAnn was still on. Callie's heart sank, and she didn't even try to convince herself that she wanted the other woman gone only to reduce the potential for divorce.

She wanted her gone, period.

She still wanted Ethan for herself.

"Let's take our drinks into the living room," Ethan said abruptly, leading the way.

Callie sat on the sofa again, drinking her lemonade more quickly and feeling foolish for caring about Ethan's life.

"I know you saw the flowers," Ethan said. "I don't know why either one of us should be embarrassed. We've moved on, haven't we? They are for LeeAnn."

"I figured. Date tonight?"

"Not exactly. Her group is playing at the Crawdad Creek Saloon, off West Street. I'm going to her concert."

Callie nodded. She didn't want to know about this. Then again, maybe she did. "Which instrument does Lee-Ann play?"

"Fiddle, and she sings backup vocals, too. River's Bend does mostly bluegrass, but every so often they play an old-style country song. They are pretty good."

Forcing a smile, Callie said, "You've always enjoyed bluegrass."

"So have you."

She shrugged.

"So come with me tonight."

Ethan couldn't have meant to say that. Callie raised her eyebrows.

He held her gaze. She could almost hear his thoughts. *Why not? We are still married.*

They were, dammit. They were still married, and she still loved him. Soon she'd go home, and she might not see him again. Ever.

Refusing to think deeper about that thought, or about the jealous curiosity that had seized her impulses, Callie smiled and shrugged again. "I'd love to hear LeeAnn play."

Chapter Nine

"Am I dressed all right?" Callie asked nervously.

Ethan didn't have to look across his car seat to know. He'd taken full notice of Callie earlier, when she'd arrived at his door. She'd worn a Western-style jean skirt and a ruffled white blouse. Her hair was down, and the hint of color she'd worn on her eyes and lips appeared nothing at all like armor.

In fact, her wearing any makeup at all showed a vulnerability. As if she was admitting that she cared what he thought. "You're gorgeous," he said quietly.

Too gorgeous. LeeAnn would be livid. But he could explain that Callie had made a special trip to Wichita just to return his toolbox, and that he hadn't felt right about booting her off his front porch. He'd thought she might appreciate the music, he'd say, and assure LeeAnn that Callie's presence was practically an accident.

What he wouldn't explain was that the evening would give him one more chance to figure out why he wasn't forgetting about Callie, and why the most exciting woman he could imagine dating wasn't erasing those old memories.

Callie smelled good, although again the effect was subtle. She hadn't sprayed on perfume or bathed in oils with an intention to entice. She'd always smelled this way. Even when she'd come home from the lab with those sharp, sterile smells clinging to her clothes, he'd hug her and catch hints of her rain-scented soap and herbal conditioner.

He ached to bury his face in her neck now.

But seducing Callie wasn't his intention, tonight. In fact, he intended only to answer some questions for himself.

They walked into the Crawdad Creek just as the band was heading for the stage. Ethan found the front-row table LeeAnn had reserved for him, helped Callie into a chair and ordered her a drink. She'd asked for a beer again. She must be nervous. Now she asked for the location of a pay phone so she could call her sisters.

He pointed toward a hallway, then got up at the same time she did. At her questioning look, he picked up the flower box. "I'm not following you. I thought I'd go give these to LeeAnn," he said.

No need to leave the thing sitting on the table, right under Callie's nose. Besides, he might be able to defuse LeeAnn's temper if he gave the flowers to her immediately.

As soon as LeeAnn saw him approach, she grabbed his arm and pulled him off to the side. "What's she doing here?"

"She brought me the toolbox I'd left at her sister's place," Ethan said. "I mentioned that I was coming here, and she said she wanted to hear you play."

LeeAnn squinted toward the audience. "She said that?"

"Sure."

"Right." LeeAnn poked a finger at his chest. "She wants you back."

If only.

"I don't think so," he said.

"You shouldn't have brought her. Are we still going dancing after the show?"

Crap. He'd forgotten his promise. He could take Callie to her car and return for LeeAnn.

But he didn't want to. "I guess not," he said. "I'm sorry. I wasn't thinking."

"Be good, Ethan."

He threw his palms up. "You know me, LeeAnn. If I meant to be anything else, I wouldn't have brought Callie here, would I? Also, she's not some new woman I've brought to make you jealous. She's my ex."

LeeAnn pouted. "Right."

Todd, the short, brawny mandolin player, walked off the stage and approached LeeAnn. "Let's do this, babe," he said. "You'll be fine."

Ethan studied Todd. Sure enough, he saw an intensity in the man's expression. LeeAnn nodded and walked onstage with him.

Until tonight, Ethan had had no idea that the guy had a crush on his girlfriend. This might be an interesting night.

The band started with a few of their new songs, and Ethan knew Callie was impressed. She bobbed her head, tapped her fingers against her beer bottle and applauded. Ethan was proud to have her sitting beside him.

He was prouder of her, sitting here responding, than of LeeAnn, playing her heart out onstage.

Ethan wasn't being honest with himself or with either woman. He still had a thing for his wife, and LeeAnn wasn't going to erase it. Even if Callie divorced him, Lee-Ann would be a consolation prize.

She shouldn't accept that status.

LeeAnn must have recognized the truth, too. She and

the mandolin player had played an entire song standing eye-to-eye, making a show of a flirtation that wowed most of the crowd. At the end, LeeAnn laughed and kissed Todd right on the mouth.

Ethan was trying to comprehend his reaction to that—amusement rather than jealousy—when Callie's chuckle snagged his attention.

She wasn't watching the drama onstage.

She was watching *him*.

"My sisters gave me a hard time on the phone," she said during a short break between songs.

"Both of them?" Ethan asked, chuckling. He'd expect Josie to tease, but not Isabel.

"Mmm-hmm. Isabel gloated because she'd already suggested that I'd be staying in Wichita longer than I thought."

Ethan kept smiling. Callie's beer had loosened her up. "What did Josie say?"

"I didn't speak to her, but I heard her humming a particular song in the background."

River's Bend started playing again, so Ethan spoke louder. "What song?"

"'Tonight's the Night.'"

The song title brought sobering thoughts to Ethan's mind.

Callie leaned forward, speaking into his ear. "They think they know me better than I know myself."

The feel of her breath on his ear distracted him plenty, but Ethan was still interested in what she'd said. He hoped her sisters did know her that well.

"When you get home, tell them I twisted your arm and made you go out with me," he said, also leaning close.

Couples had begun to dance between the tables, and Callie watched wistfully. In taking the Blume girls' entire education into her hands, Ella had done well. But she'd either forgotten about music, or she'd decided it wasn't worth her time. The girls hadn't learned to appreciate music until they were old enough to battle Ella.

Callie might feel the influence of the music as much as anyone, but she contented herself with watching the dancing. They'd always talked about taking lessons.

He wished they had. He wanted to dance with her. Maybe he should just ask. She moved well enough sitting in her seat. She'd do fine.

Ethan remembered where he was, glanced at the stage and discovered LeeAnn watching him. She might have flaunted her interest in the mandolin player, but Ethan hadn't intended to reveal his attraction to Callie.

Maybe he was doing that now, however unintentionally.

Maybe he should admit to himself that the failed relationship was his with LeeAnn.

Maybe he should get Callie out of here.

He glanced at her, considering how he should suggest their departure, and noticed her eyes and lips.

Really noticed them.

Everything else be damned, he wanted to kiss her here and now. Whatever was prompting her resistance to him, it wasn't that she was involved with some other man. That much was obvious. And he suspected that she wanted him as much as he wanted her. "Ready to go?" he asked.

She was halfway out of her seat before she remembered to act surprised. "Now?" she asked huskily.

He didn't buy it. He simply smiled at her, took her hand and led her from the club. He'd talk to LeeAnn later, but he suspected that Todd would take advantage of this situation and stick very near to his fiddle-playing friend. Maybe they'd go dancing together.

Callie stayed quiet on the way home. He was glad. He wanted her too intensely to chat or laugh or pretend or do anything but want her. At home, he parked in his garage and got out, closing the garage door and walking into his house. He didn't mention Callie's rental car, still at the curb, or the idea of her returning to Augusta tonight.

He simply entered his kitchen, hoping to heck she was following him.

She was.

He dropped his keys and wallet on the counter, then took her purse and set it there, too. Finally, he looped his arms behind Callie's knees and waist, picking her up to carry her straight through to his bed.

No words.

No spoken questions.

No hesitations.

Somewhere between the kitchen and his bed, he touched his mouth to hers, but restrained his full passion so he could avoid bumping into walls and furniture.

Callie slid a hand through his hair, holding his face captive, and kissed him more deeply. Her parted lips and evocative murmurs made him wonder how he would find his way.

He managed.

He eased Callie across his mattress and followed without ever allowing a space between them. He claimed her mouth again, kissing her with an eager heart and a sensual tongue. He claimed her body just as urgently, unbuttoning her shirt and sliding a hand beneath her bra to peel it upward. Palming her breasts possessively.

Needfully.

Leaving no room for regrets or goodbyes.

He satisfied himself for long minutes, loving her with

his lips and hands. Fingering her nipples to peaks that were darker and sexier than he remembered. Plundering her mouth with an enthusiasm he'd never forgotten.

When Callie shifted her hips beneath his, not just adjusting to his hardened length but also beginning a seductive motion, he finally spoke. "I want to make love to you," he said.

She nodded.

"I haven't had sex in two years," he said, grinning fleetingly at her gasp. "Is protection necessary from your end?"

He wouldn't have asked anyone else. Condom use would have been a no-brainer. But since he'd met Callie eleven years ago, she had been his only lover. Until two years ago, he'd been her only for all time. Since she was infertile, unprotected sex posed no risks, unless something had changed for her between then and now.

By God, he wanted to *know* if it had.

She shook her head.

Ethan saw beauty and pain in her simple gesture. He trembled when he kissed her again, more tenderly. He helped her remove her blouse, her skirt, her under things, taking his time to touch her more patiently.

He didn't have to rush, or worry that she'd change her mind. They'd already spoken of their intent.

She helped him undress, too, kissing him all the while, and letting him feel the incredible sweetness of her desire.

Then he pushed inside her.

She felt so right.

Ethan was glad he'd waited all this time. Until he knew for certain that his time with Callie was finished, he'd wanted to be faithful to her.

When it came right down to it, he'd never wanted her to doubt his deep loyalty.

"You feel so good," he whispered against her neck as he let her body adjust to his size and length.

"You do, too," she said, but tears were beginning to spill from her luminous gray eyes.

He felt that intensity of emotion, too.

He kissed her cheeks, tasting the salt and licking it, trying to make her laugh. When she did, he ravaged her mouth again, turning up the heat of eroticism to erase her tears in another way.

He lowered his mouth to her breasts, kissing and licking her there, too, reveling in their responsiveness. As he focused on other things, trying to ensure her complete arousal, she grasped his buttocks and shoved her hips upward, taking him fully inside. Then she slid away from him.

Again, she drove her hips forward. Again, she slipped away. This time she moaned her pleasure. The next time she hitched her breath and sighed.

For a time, Ethan enjoyed the lazy sensation of allowing her to lead. Until he forgot about her breasts and her lips and fell into her rhythms. He took control then, loving her until he felt ready to go. Then he stared into her wet eyes, listened to her breaths and gauged her readiness.

When it was time, he took her legs and wrapped them around his torso. He drove deeper and faster, allowing the urgency to take over until her last moan became a shout and their bodies shuddered from the long, high release.

"Wow, Callie."

"Don't talk," she said. "Just let this be what it is."

He wondered what she thought this was, exactly.

He wanted to tell her he'd been wrong. That no matter how awful their fighting had become, he shouldn't have left her. That he might have become temporarily disenchanted by her fierce emotions, but he'd loved her for them, too.

Maybe he should wait, to tell her that. Maybe he should begin to prove it first.

Already, as he rested his head against her chest and listened to her heartbeat slowing, he was beginning to want her again.

It had been a long time.

When he skittered his kisses down her flat abdomen to her hip bones and beyond, she didn't allow him to stay any longer than one very intimate kiss.

Laughing, she grabbed his shoulders and pulled him next to her. "No. Not that," she said, then rolled around on top of him. "This."

They made love again, and Ethan thrilled at knowing he was loving the same woman he'd loved since he was old enough to make a mature choice.

Shy Callie had never been shy in bed. She made love like a smart girl who knew how things worked and never let that knowledge get in the way of her fun.

Sweet mercy, he loved her.

"Callie, I need to tell you something," he said when they were relaxing again, this time in each other's arms.

"No. Talk isn't necessary. We just need to get this out of our systems," she said matter-of-factly.

Ethan chuckled, then sobered. "You really think that's possible?"

In answer, she slid a hand behind his neck, pulling him forward. "Maybe. You never know. One more time might do the trick."

He pulled away slightly, studying her.

She was serious.

As Ethan kissed her, he allowed himself to follow her

lead again, knowing for certain that this time, she was wrong. She might not recognize it yet, but Ethan believed they would reconcile.

She acted as if she'd forgiven him for being a man, and for living on after her mother had died.

Even for leaving.

And he'd realized that his strong attraction to her had as much to do with her complexity as her beauty. He wouldn't lose sight of that fact again. The very intensity that had driven him away from Callie two years ago had made her unforgettable.

AFTER HANGING UP the phone in Ethan's kitchen, Callie felt better. Luke had been fine in her absence. Josie might have bantered more than she'd talked, but her responses assured Callie that all was well at the apartment.

Callie hadn't meant to stay, but Isabel's solemn assurances during last evening's phone conversation had made her feel comfortable about being out late. And when things had stayed hot with Ethan until she was too tired to think about leaving, she'd chosen to stay.

Just as she'd chosen to make love to him, these last few times.

How could she have forgotten how much she enjoyed sex?

Whenever she'd thought about her past with Ethan, she'd remembered the kissing and touching more than the actual act. Maybe because the infertility problems had made it feel too forced, toward the end. Or maybe because, in her mind, she'd relinquished that part of life forever.

If her relationship with Ethan couldn't survive, she'd reasoned, how on earth could she expect another to work?

So she'd basked in the delicious sensations of her body's pairing with Ethan's, refusing to succumb to guilt about her time away from Luke or about Ethan's relationship with LeeAnn.

Last night's lovemaking had been his choice initially, not hers. She hoped he'd made it consciously.

Now she turned around, noting her purse, his keys and his wallet in the place on the counter where he must always leave his things.

The same place where LeeAnn's flowers had sat just yesterday evening. That memory made her heart ache, so she lurched away from the counter and padded past the kitchen table, glancing at the clutter and feeling like a snooping houseguest—wanting to see, but guilty about her curiosity.

She wasn't his wife anymore. Not really.

Her pulse raced even more when she neared Ethan's bedroom. Callie paused, hand to heart, and tried to calm herself. She hoped he was still sleeping. She'd go in and hang his bathrobe on its peg, then gather her scattered clothes. She might manage to escape without waking him. At least for this morning, she'd escape his scrutiny and impossible expectations.

Avoiding those conversations had been easy last night. They'd been naked. Aroused.

Evasion seemed tougher this morning.

She stepped into the room and smiled at his sleeping form. They'd been awake so late. They'd made love again about an hour ago. After that last time, he'd gone to sleep.

She hadn't. She'd lain awake, waiting until it was late enough to call and check on Luke, and worrying about how to handle the situation this morning.

Callie hung up Ethan's sleek green robe. Returning to his bedside, she scooped her panties off the floor. Vulnerable in her nudity, she slipped them on, then hunted for her bra.

She saw it beneath Ethan's foot, sticking out from beneath the sheets. She inched toward the bed, wondering if she should even try to get it.

Did she have a choice?

She could leave without it and risk having him return her lingerie at some inopportune time, or she could try. Grabbing the strap, she pulled gently, then watched Ethan slide a muscular arm toward her side of the bed.

Oh, no! Wasn't he sleeping? His face was turned away from her, so she couldn't tell.

As soon as she'd had the thought, he patted the mattress and turned his head toward the side where she'd slept.

Worried that he might note her absence and wake more fully, Callie hastened around and lowered herself beside his hand, closing her eyes and feigning sleep.

His fingers scraped through her hair, then he moaned. He must be in a light sleep cycle.

She lay still, feeling very much the way she did when Luke woke at night and needed the comfort of her presence. As if she was pacifying him, waiting until it was safe to return to bed or finish washing the dishes.

Or, in Ethan's case, to return to her Denver life with the son he didn't recognize as his.

When Ethan grew still again, Callie watched him. For the first time in a long time, she could look as much as she wanted. Even with his eyes closed, his face showed character. His strong jaw had a thick shadow this morning—he'd missed his shave last night—and only a trace of a dimple showed. His dark brown hair was mussed. His shoulders were broad, very tanned for mid-June. He must still run, sometimes, with his shirt off.

Beneath the blanket, his torso tapered down to the smaller, flat plane of his waist, then rounded out to buttocks shaped well from his years of running.

Appearances aside, she loved this man. She'd never lost that love. She'd simply lost faith in her ability to succeed at the marriage.

She'd always been an outsider. When she was very little, Callie had disliked the curious glances at the grocer or fabric counter in town. A few times, an ignorant child or thoughtless adult had commented on her homemade clothes or well-worn shoes.

More than her sisters, perhaps, Callie had felt the severe weight of her family's differences. Even then, she'd sensed that Ella wasn't emotionally stable. That she should have been trying harder to keep her children connected to the world.

For a time, Ethan had helped Callie connect to the world in a social sense.

When her mother died, Callie had been devastated. Perhaps she had let Ella's old beliefs rule her thoughts for a while. Perhaps she'd forgotten that Ethan had had her best interests at heart, too.

As she did his, right now.

This morning, she couldn't allow him to say anything about love or commitment or even regret without first telling him about his son.

So she would return to Augusta and figure out how to tell him the truth. Then she'd phone him, offering to meet him at a time when he wasn't enticingly naked and warm with sleep.

He rolled over onto his side, facing her.

She noticed his arousal first. That caused her stomach to flip and her heart to flutter. Then she realized she could access her bra.

She sat up and leaned down to grab it, but Ethan reached out to run a hand along the curve of her hip.

She folded the bra into her palm and met his open-eyed gaze. "Morning," he said, rich humor deepening his voice and lighting his eyes.

"You awake?" she asked stupidly, knowing he was but requiring a moment to adjust to the idea.

He grabbed her shoulders, tumbled her down and rolled on top of her. "Every part of me is awake," he murmured. Then he bucked his hips to show off again.

She chuckled. She'd always loved that part of his personality.

He felt so good. Hot and firm in all the right places. Lord help her, Callie wanted to feel those sensations one more time. She could handle anything but talk.

"I thought I'd dreamed last night," he said against her ear, then backed away to gaze into her eyes.

She smiled, shy in the dim light. Closing her eyes, she reached up to kiss Ethan's jaw. Allowing herself to concentrate on her sensuality. Hoping to rid him of his desire for talk.

He slid warm hands to the curve of her waist, then fingered her panties. "Hey! How did these get here?" he teased as he tugged them down her legs. Dropping them beside the bed, he took hold of her hands, discovered the bra and got rid of that, too.

"Don't be in such a rush to go," he growled. Then he adjusted her hips, and with a smooth movement pushed inside her. Showing her the reward for sticking around.

At first, they didn't kiss on the mouth. They hadn't

done that in the mornings, Callie remembered. The sex had always been fast and geared toward satiating desire before they showered and dressed for the day.

It had always made her frantic to brush her teeth and enjoy a really uninhibited good-morning kiss.

Ethan had rushed for the toothbrush, too, although he'd always added a quick shave so he didn't scrape her face with his whiskers.

This morning, after a few mind-numbing moments, Ethan kissed her anyway. Callie didn't worry about scratches or bad breath or what might happen in twenty minutes. She simply kissed him back.

Later on, she dozed, and awoke with a start when she heard the buzz of his electric shaver in the adjacent bathroom. Finally, she grabbed her bra and hooked it around herself. Panties came next, then she located her blouse and skirt and had those on before Ethan had finished shaving.

With his appetite sated, he'd probably be more in the mood for talk—about what had happened here, what it meant and what they should do about it.

She needed to leave, allowing herself time to plan a much-needed conversation.

"In a hurry?" he asked when he returned a half second later.

"I have to go," she said. "My sisters might worry."

He handed her a wrapped toothbrush, chuckling at her reaction. "I thought you got hold of Josie this morning," he said.

Forgetting about the shave and toothbrush, and whatever they implied, Callie wondered how much he had heard. "You were awake?"

"Sort of. I heard you walk into the kitchen, and I thought I heard you say something to Josie about the baby." He shook his head. "Was that a dream?"

Callie tried not to panic. "No, I called her to check on things. I still need to get going."

He shrugged. "Sure."

He began to dress while she hustled past him to use the toothbrush and stare in the mirror at her tangled hair.

"Those are clean towels if you want to take the time to shower," he hollered through the door.

"No thanks."

She washed her face, noticing the thick red towels folded on a metal shelf above his sink. They were the same brand and color she had at home. Isabel had given them a set that last Christmas they'd been together.

He must have searched Wichita for them, wishing to duplicate them here. Somehow this morning, just knowing that made Callie sad.

But how could a breakup be anything but sad?

Callie used her fingers to comb her hair, then emerged from the bathroom and watched Ethan go in again. That was typical for them, too. Neither had wanted to monopolize the bathroom, so they'd taken short turns. It was amazing how quickly they had reclaimed their routines.

Callie sat on the end of his bed to finish getting dressed. He came out again before she'd had time to put on her second shoe. Or to holler a goodbye and escape all that talk.

When she stood up, fully dressed with shoes and composure in place, he kissed her again—a really good, loving morning kiss that made her feel soft and spineless again.

"Last night was great, Cal," he whispered into her neck.

She stepped away and nodded. "Let's not talk about it," she said. Her small voice sounded unconvincing, even to her own ears.

"You've got to be kidding," he said. "I need to tell you

so much." He paused, nodding as if very certain about what else he required. "I want to spend time with you today."

Callie sat back down on the bed, staring at him as she made a quick decision. "I need to go," she said. "I really do. Do you think you could come to Isabel's around noon? I have something to tell you, too."

But it isn't at all what you must be expecting to hear.

"I'll be there," he promised. "Should I dress to work?"

Callie shook her head. "Most of the work is done. The inspector will be out on Tuesday or Wednesday. We'll have Izzy in her house later this week."

"Wow. That's great," he said, but he raked a hand through his hair.

Maybe he was as surprised as she was by the timing of what had happened last night. In another week or two, she would have been gone. They would have resumed their separate lives, living them as they had before the flood had brought them together again.

The future would be different now. Ethan would know about his son. Callie didn't know how the rest would play out. The timing might be considered very lucky or quite unlucky.

Depending on one's perspective.

"Sure it is," she said. "Izzy is excited about being home." As she spoke, Callie headed toward the door.

Ethan followed her, but veered off into his kitchen. Callie thought she might make it outside before he finished whatever he was doing, or said anything else.

But he appeared immediately with her purse. Of course, he'd put it on his kitchen counter last night. She'd seen it this morning.

She opened the front door. He handed the purse across.

She reached for the screen door handle. He took hold of her hand, holding her captive as he gazed at her and said it.

"I love you, Callie."

She blinked.

He let go of her.

She didn't repeat the words, respond outwardly to his confession or even wait for Ethan's reaction to her lack of response.

She simply pushed open the screen door, and left.

Chapter Ten

A half hour later, Callie let herself into Josie's apartment and realized no one was home. She was glad. As much as she wanted to see Luke and talk to her sisters, she also needed time to herself.

In the shower, she lingered under the hot spray to assuage a few extra-sore muscles. When she found herself reliving the sensuality of last night and this morning, she cut off the water and stepped out.

She dressed in white jean shorts, a sleeveless cotton shirt in deep cinnamon red, and leather sandals. Perhaps she was dressing for Ethan. Hadn't she always coveted the feel of his eyes on her? In her younger years, she'd needed to hear him say that she was pretty to believe it.

Or maybe today, she simply wanted to create an optimistic tone. Her thoughts were so jumbled. She knew only that she wanted to believe that this afternoon wouldn't be such a great big deal. She'd simply neglected to tell him one minor detail: he had a son.

Her son. Luke.

Which was without doubt a great big deal.

He'd have every right to be furious.

As Callie recombed her hair, she tried to compose a

mental script. What could she possibly say to Ethan to help him handle emotions that were sure to be powerful? How could she nurse him toward healing even as she carved a wound into his chest with her news?

She spoke her half of the imagined conversation into the mirror, wavering between the blunt truth and other, less painful versions.

Under the circumstances, I wasn't sure you would even want to know. Remember LeeAnn? You told me you were happy with your new life.

I didn't trust you. I couldn't risk losing my baby.

You didn't want me. So you couldn't have your child.

Damn. It all brought pain. And last night, he'd surely shown that he wanted her.

Sidetracked by different thoughts, Callie put on only enough makeup to feel polished, and found herself smiling into the mirror. The most private parts of her still thrummed with energy. When she finished applying mascara, however, she peered into the mirror and felt as fake as the blush on her cheeks. She couldn't exist long in this confused state. She needed to put her faith in the truth and let her future settle however it would.

Then she'd simply deal with it.

At Isabel's house, Callie found Josie loading the kitchen with groceries. Luke was on the floor behind her, chasing around a rolling can of applesauce. Callie scooped him into her arms and hugged him. "Did he eat yet this morning?" she asked Josie.

"Sure. He drank some milk from a sippy cup and ate some of my Malt-O-Meal."

"You gave him chocolate cereal for breakfast?" Callie asked.

"He can't have that?"

Callie eyed Luke, who squirmed to get loose and looked absolutely no worse for wear. She returned him to the floor and admitted to herself that she was reacting to everything with alarm, still anticipating what might happen later today.

"Did you have a good time in Wichita?" Josie asked, her face suspiciously expressionless as she transferred canned goods from a paper sack to the pantry.

"Yep. Where's Isabel?" Callie kept her tone neutral.

Josie stood up, can of corn in hand, and leaned against the counter to study Callie. "She took the paper towels downstairs."

Isabel walked in a moment later, and Callie nodded a greeting. Her middle sister must have grasped the mood of the moment, too. She stood next to Josie and stared.

"I'm telling Ethan about Luke today."

Her sisters were smart enough to contain their cheers and "I-told-you-so's." "It's that time, huh?" Josie asked softly.

"Guess so. I can't do this to him," Callie said. "Another guy, maybe. Ethan doesn't deserve it."

"I think you're right to tell him," Isabel said. "He'll be a wonderful dad."

Callie nodded.

Both of her sisters looked sympathetic.

Callie wondered if a person could explode with worry.

"So, help me," she demanded. "I told him to be here around noon. How should I handle it? Any wise advice?"

She glanced from Isabel's to Josie's face and back.

"*You,* Callie, the oldest and bossiest sister, are asking for *our* opinions?" Josie asked.

Leave it to Josie to tease.

Callie ignored the jab. "No. I'm begging for them."

Isabel chuckled. "Make him comfortable first," she said. "Feed him lunch and set a tone of friendliness."

Right. She'd thought of that. Callie nodded, encouraging further advice.

"Noon's too early to get him drunk," Josie said, grinning. "But keep the mood light. Tell a few jokes, give him some chocolate to boost his endorphins."

Her sisters certainly weren't reacting as if this was a great big deal. Callie relaxed. Maybe it would be all right.

"Hey!" Isabel said. "He wasn't here for my housewarming celebration, so let's have another. We can make the deli chicken into a sandwich spread, maybe cut up some fresh veggies and serve iced coffee. Josie and I can stay a moment, then we'll disappear so you can talk."

Party or not, Ethan would be angry after hearing the news. She'd also be upset, and she didn't want her little boy to see her arguing with Ethan. "Should I keep Luke here when you leave?" Callie asked.

"You *are* nervous," Isabel said. "Yes. Luke needs to be here. Ethan will want to hold him and get used to the idea. Josie and I will be at her place, only a phone call away if you want us to come get the baby."

Moments later, Callie telephoned Ethan let him know that her invitation included lunch. She spoke quickly, stating facts in what she hoped was a calm voice. Then she said goodbye and hung up.

Callie spent the rest of the morning playing with Luke and supervising her sisters as they bustled around preparing the special meal.

In no time, Ethan was at the door.

Izzy welcomed him inside and disappeared into the kitchen to set out lunch. Josie teased Ethan about how he was showing up wanting food again, then she took him on a quick tour of Isabel's nearly finished house.

Callie simply tried to talk and walk without screaming or stumbling or running off with her baby.

Lunch went well. Josie had Ethan laughing, telling him about a house she'd done recently whose owners reminded her of a husband-and-wife version of Laurel and Hardy.

They were all getting ready to eat a slice of store-bought chocolate cake—thank heaven her sisters had gone to the supermarket this morning—when someone knocked on the front door.

"I don't know who that could be." Isabel frowned as she pushed away from the table and got up. "Roger and the kids were going to the lumber yard this afternoon."

A moment later, she appeared in the kitchen with LeeAnn following.

Ethan stood up. "What are you doing here?"

"Looking for you. I figured you'd come to one of the sisters' places again. You're spending a lot of time here."

"But how did you find it?"

"Phone book." She smiled. "I remembered the sisters were Blumes, found two addresses and got lucky with the first." As LeeAnn surveyed the table, her gaze lingered on the bowl of yellow roses, then on the blue glass dessert plates, still pretty with untouched wedges of cake.

Obviously, she'd noticed the celebratory mood. Lord knew what she would make of it. "Isn't this lovely?" she asked, her voice and eyes hard.

"We're celebrating Isabel's return home," Ethan said in an equally crisp tone.

"I see," LeeAnn said. "Well, *I* went by your house to ask why you'd left early last night. You didn't answer your door or phone, of course, so I figured you were here again." She shrugged. "I believe we need to talk."

"Yes, we do," Ethan said. He shook his head. "But not here and now."

"Why don't we all sit and have dessert," Isabel said, grabbing an extra plate and moving a slice of cake onto it. "Would you like some cake, er…" her voice trailed off and she glanced at Callie "…LeeAnn?"

"Sorry," Ethan said. "I thought you knew. Isabel and Josie, this is LeeAnn Chambers. LeeAnn, Callie's sisters. Isabel is the one with the cake. Josie is sitting."

After they'd all nodded to one another, he turned his attention to Luke, who'd been buckled into a booster seat at the end of the table. Luke was content with a cup of juice, a bowl of cubed chicken and a piece of zwieback toast.

Callie hoped he stayed that way.

"And this is Luke, the apple of everyone's eye," Ethan added, smiling.

The baby kept his sippy cup attached to his mouth, but he stared at LeeAnn.

Who gaped at him. Then she bent down to study his eyes. "Oh, my *God!*" she exclaimed.

"What!" Callie jumped up and ran around the table, examining her son in alarm. "Is something wrong?"

Still crouching, LeeAnn smiled up at Callie, eyebrows raised. Then she stood again and smirked at Ethan. She made a show of reaching up to touch his hair, so dark a brown it was often mistaken for black. "Your coloring isn't all that common, is it?" she said. "That thick, dark hair and those caramel-brown eyes." She shook her head. "Not common at all."

Then she eyed the baby again. She touched the thick,

dark hair. Peered into the caramelly brown eyes. And nodded. "You didn't tell me you had a son, Ethan."

"I DON'T," ETHAN SAID immediately.

Then he remembered Callie's reaction mere seconds ago, when she'd been worried that something might be wrong with the little boy. He remembered Luke's birthday last month. Callie had taken him to the park, hadn't she? She'd helped him open his first wrapped present.

He remembered Callie telephoning her sisters last night, and again this morning. Just as any worried mother would do, when leaving her young son in the care of others.

Ethan eyed Callie, still standing near the boy. When she met his gaze, her face froze into an expression of apology.

She gave a slight nod.

Ethan watched what happened next in the kitchen as if it was taking place in slow motion. Isabel and Josie started carrying the cake-laden dessert plates to the sink. LeeAnn stood with her arms crossed in front of her, watching Callie. Callie herself lifted her hands to her head, watching both him and Luke as if she expected one of them to disintegrate.

That's when Ethan shifted his focus to the little boy. He stepped around to Luke's booster seat, slipped to his knees in front of the baby and pulled the chair away from the table.

Needing to get a really good look.

He studied the dark hair. It was similar to his own and his father's, wasn't it? He'd told Callie that once, but he'd forgotten now how she'd responded.

He noted a pair of slanted, golden-brown eyes—those were from Mom's side—and he saw the dimpled grin.

And he *felt* it.

This was his son.

The baby didn't act as if he minded being watched. He drank from the yellow plastic cup and stared at Ethan, too young yet to know anything about polite social distance. Then he lifted the cup toward Ethan, as if offering to share.

Smiling sadly, Ethan said, "No, Luke. I don't want a drink."

Son.

He couldn't bring himself to say it. Not without choking up. Would he ever have known about this boy? Would Callie have told him?

No.

No. He didn't think so.

She'd had plenty of time to tell him. She'd been here in Augusta for almost two months, and she hadn't. Hell, she'd known about the baby for almost two years—since he'd left Denver, for mercy's sake.

And she hadn't told him.

Despondence settled in Ethan's chest. He'd thought last night had meant something. He'd thought they would destroy those divorce papers this afternoon, and begin to solve the problem of their separate living arrangements.

When Ethan would have stood to face Callie and say *something,* the little boy caught his attention.

"Dee?" Luke said, and lifted his bowl.

Apparently, he was pleased to have finished his meal.

Luke was such a smart kid. Such a charming one. Why hadn't Ethan figured it out?

Ethan inhaled deeply, softening a reaction too severe to display in front of the child. "I do see," he said, and spent another few minutes reacquainting himself with the little boy he'd already begun to love.

Eventually, he realized that the sounds in the kitchen had changed. No constant squeak-thump of sneakers on clean tile. No clank and clatter of dishes being stacked. He glanced backward, noting that Callie had joined her sisters at the sink. They stood in a group, arms encircling one another as they whispered.

Ethan sneered when he realized that even LeeAnn had joined their group.

As if she was one of *them.*

Ha! He'd always felt a kinship with them, too. From the first day Callie had brought her sisters to Wichita to meet him, he'd liked all three of those girls. But in that moment, Ethan realized that the Blume sisters had conspired against him. Even Josie, his buddy. And loyal Isabel.

The baby chuckled, clearly finding the women's behavior odd. That caught Ethan's attention and helped him gain perspective. He felt proud of his boy's affability.

Proud of his son, period.

Vaguely, Ethan registered the sound of footsteps again. Josie hollered something, then the front door slammed.

Ethan didn't care about anything but that slam.

He knew he was alone with his son and his son's mother. The time for questions and answers had come.

He could control his temper. Anger would gain him nothing and might cost him dearly. He'd take his cues from too-cool Callie, who had certainly kept her composure during the past two months while she'd masqueraded as her own son's devoted aunt.

While she'd lied to him, repeatedly.

This was *their* son—the baby she had wanted so badly.

But so had he.

So had he, damn it!

When Callie approached, Ethan stepped sideways, hoping to heaven she wasn't planning to touch him. His emotions were too volatile, and he didn't know whether he'd laugh next, or succumb to some darker emotion.

Rage. Remorse.

Either of those responses would surely be reasonable.

But Callie stepped past him, unfastening the baby's seat buckle and picking him up.

Ethan had always suspected that Callie would be an overprotective mother. Way back when, he'd figured he'd have to convince her to let their child play team sports or ride around the neighborhood on a bicycle. Now, Ethan knew he'd have to fight for time with his son.

And he *would*.

He scowled as he watched her cuddle the boy to her chest. She carried him across to the sink, then wetted a washcloth and wiped the baby's face and hands.

He'd watched her wash Luke before, several times. Yet he felt as if he didn't know her, even after having loved her for most of his adult life.

Even after rekindling those feelings with her last night.

After last night, her treachery felt monstrous.

He expected her to turn toward him and make another composed recitation of the facts. Hadn't she always fought that way?

But she stunned him by returning to put the little boy in his arms. "Luke's yours, Ethan. He's your son."

He knew.

And he was off balance again, confused by Callie's generosity.

"I know." He held Luke tight enough to satisfy his ravenous heart, but then moved him away so he could look at him again.

Unbelievable. The little boy did look just like him.

He'd been foolish to miss it before. He wouldn't have, except that he'd known Callie wasn't pregnant at the time of their separation. He'd been the one to hold her the last time she'd learned she wasn't pregnant.

"How?" he asked abruptly.

"This might take a while," Callie said. "Come in here where we can sit comfortably."

She led him into Isabel's living room. After they'd sat at opposite ends of the new sofa, Callie said, "You left when I was still an active patient at the reproductive clinic, remember?"

Luke squirmed, so Ethan shifted him to his knees and held on to both hands, bouncing him gently and making him chortle.

"I thought we'd exhausted those options," he said, bouncing higher as Luke laughed louder. "Trying that way and failing repeatedly had cost us a lot more than money."

Callie nodded. "You'd given up hope. I hadn't."

"So you went to the clinic after I'd left you?" he asked. It was a stupid question. Of course she had. But he needed to know exactly how everything had played out.

"Dat-dat," Luke said, and Ethan realized he was forgetting to bounce. He pulled the boy into his arms again and stood up, too nervous to sit. He paced the floor, jiggling the boy just hard enough to make him laugh again.

Callie stood, too, but she remained near the sofa and held Ethan's gaze, just as she had in the kitchen a few moments ago.

Except now, tears were rolling down her cheeks. "Six weeks later, I went back."

"And you gave yourself the shots afterward? You went for all those blood tests and ultrasounds, alone?"

She nodded. "Sometimes Patty from the lab went with me."

"Why would you go, when we had separated?"

He felt Luke patting his cheeks and realized his face was wet, too.

"I hoped that one last try might be the one that saved us." She paused to brush away her tears. "So I did try. And the blood tests were all positive and the ultrasounds showed one growing baby." She shrugged.

Then she glanced at Luke and nodded.

She'd expected the pregnancy to save their marriage? That was a huge expectation to put on an unborn child. Ethan would have told her that, then.

Now, telling her was pointless.

"You didn't think you could call to tell me?" he asked.

She shook her head.

"Sweet mercy."

Unexpectedly, the baby gripped Ethan's cheeks to turn his face. "Dat," he said, pointing toward Isabel's picture window. Outside, a little blue swing swayed gently in the breeze. Ethan had seen it earlier, when he'd driven up. He'd smiled at the thought of Callie's nephew enjoying it.

Callie sighed. "He wants to swing."

Ethan knew.

He looked at Luke, but spoke for Callie's benefit. "I can take you outside." He paused for a moment before adding, "Son." He paused for a longer moment. "But tell your mother to come with us so we can finish talking."

Callie walked out to the yard with them, then helped buckle their little boy into the swing. She walked around to stand behind Luke, once again helping Ethan push the baby.

Luke was just as happy as he'd been the last time they'd done a similar thing.

But *they* were so completely different.

That day at the City Park, he'd spent his time alternating between wanting Callie, enjoying the day and feeling guilty about LeeAnn.

He'd had the slight hope that he and Callie would be a couple again.

Now, that was surely impossible.

"You should have told me after that first blood test came back positive," he said.

"At that point, I was hoping you'd come home on your own," Callie said. "I thought my news would be a happy surprise for you, when you did."

"But I didn't come home."

She angled her chin. "Nope."

"I would have, if I'd known."

Callie stopped pushing Luke. "I know you would have," she said, and glanced at the baby. "For him."

He shook his head. "For both of you."

She made a wry face. She might not believe him, but he'd never stopped loving her.

Now he knew.

Love wasn't always enough.

She hadn't trusted him then—not completely. She'd always had the worry that he would leave her. Ella had instilled that thought deeply into her soul.

Now, Ethan realized that he couldn't trust Callie.

The two of them had lost that inherent attitude of fairness toward each other that every couple needed. Maybe they'd never really had it. Callie wouldn't have learned about it from her mother.

And maybe he'd expected too much of himself. He was

a man, and quite human. When he hadn't been able to fix Callie's problems, he had left.

"He's my son, Callie. That's too big a secret to keep. You should have told me. Especially after last night." The last few words faded to a whisper. The magnitude of her duplicity overwhelmed him.

Her actions were unforgivable.

"I was going to. Today."

Ethan kept swinging Luke, thinking. Maybe she had been planning to tell him. She had asked him to come to Augusta to talk.

But maybe she hadn't.

He needed time to figure things out.

"I want to spend the afternoon alone with Luke," he said abruptly, stopping the swing and unbuckling the seat belt without help.

She frowned as she watched him lift the boy into his arms. "To do what?"

"Nothing, really," Ethan said. "I just need time to adjust to the idea. Maybe we'll go to the park again."

She lifted a hand to her head and stared at her little boy—at *his* little boy. "It's pretty hot today," she said. "It must be in the mideighties already."

"I'll keep him in the shade and leave if he acts distressed. You know I have a legal right to my son, Cal. Be reasonable."

Still, she hesitated.

Maybe she thought he'd run off to some unknown place with Luke, keeping their son to himself. She should know better. That wasn't his style.

He hadn't thought it was hers.

"I'll stay right here in town, I promise," he said. "If it makes you feel more comfortable, you can drop us off at the park and pick us up in a few hours." He shook his head. "Don't worry that I'll run off with him."

She gasped. "That's not what I'm worried about at all."

"Isn't it?"

"No. We just need to talk."

"Sometimes all the talk in the world will get you nowhere. We proved that."

Callie's eyes were too bright. She wasn't normally an easy crier. She'd ranted and worried and fidgeted at various times, but she'd only cried when she felt hopeless.

"All right," she said. "Let's transfer his car seat to your car. It isn't necessary for me to drop you off. I know Luke will be safe with you."

Good. Another act of generosity. He and Callie hadn't succeeded as a married couple, but perhaps they could be good parents separately. Ethan held Callie's gaze. "I'll have him home no later than five o'clock."

She closed her eyes, gave a nod and opened them again. "Okay. And you're right," she said. "We can be reasonable. And if we put our minds to doing what's right for Luke, we'll get through this."

Hopeful words, and yet she'd sounded miserable.

That's when it struck Ethan.

She lived in Denver.

He lived here.

They would each want to spend every available minute with their son. Somehow. In that instant, he understood a hint of what she must have gone through.

Yet her choices had proved her level of doubt. She hadn't given him a chance to prove himself. She'd simply decided for him. "Right," he said, pretending confidence. "We'll figure it out."

Chapter Eleven

"Josie, look out for that car!" Callie shouted, glaring from the truck's side window as a bald man in a sporty yellow convertible whipped between lanes and came too close to the side where Luke slept in his car seat.

"Which one?" Josie asked.

"All of them!" Callie said quite seriously, causing both Josie and Isabel to chuckle.

Josie's eyes met Callie's in her rearview mirror. "Come on, Cal. I'm following your explicit instructions—slow on corners, slower in traffic, and I'm heeding the posted signs. I even stayed under the speed limit on the highway."

"By two miles per hour."

Isabel glanced around from her spot in Josie's front passenger seat. "Our kid sister's doing fine," she said. "I think you're just worried about leaving Luke with Ethan again."

"Sure I am," Callie admitted. "I'm handing my son over to a man who has every right to hate me."

"For two hours, while we shop for Izzy's new range," Josie said, braking for a red light. "Besides, Ethan doesn't hate you. Didn't you say that Wednesday evening, he invited you to come in?"

"Yes."

"See?"

Callie sighed. "We talked about Luke, Josie. Ethan hadn't realized he was ready to walk. We spent an hour sitting on the floor, encouraging him to toddle between us."

"Did he walk on his own?" Isabel asked, smiling.

Callie grinned, too. "He took five steps once. Another time, he lurched off toward the sofa and caught himself. He's on his way."

"Then your time together was well spent," Izzy said.

Maybe. But their time together had been only for the sake of the child. Ethan's tone with Callie was too polite, his expression too distant. And neither of them had mentioned last Saturday night. Ethan's vow of love appeared to have been forgotten.

Exactly as Callie had expected. It was one of the reasons she'd wanted to tell him about Luke before he professed his love for her. To save them the hassle of remembering words spoken too quickly, about feelings that weren't based on complete honesty.

As her sisters watched traffic, waiting for the light to change, Callie lost herself in the same circle of thoughts she'd been having for seven days.

It was Saturday. Exactly a week and only a week since the night she'd spent with Ethan.

So much had changed and so much hadn't.

Isabel had returned to her house on Tuesday. She had contacted her clients and started taking orders again for her specialty quilts and baskets.

Yet Callie and Luke were still camped out in Josie's living room. Although Callie and Ethan had talked about Luke every day that week, they hadn't managed to talk about what they should *do* about him. Even if Ethan's feelings for Callie had changed, they still had to make some decisions together.

But she feared the discussions. Feared the upcoming changes. Forcing the conversation would surely rush her to an unwanted end.

Adding to her turmoil, Stan had called twice yesterday, reminding her that she'd promised to be at work on Monday.

She couldn't return to Denver that soon. Stan might think the lab was in peril of falling apart—hell, maybe it was—but her life was already in shambles. She wouldn't be worth a beaker of air if she returned to Denver now.

She was glad Ethan knew about Luke.

But she wasn't.

She was glad to have made love to Ethan last week—really glad. But she wasn't. His coldness hurt.

She'd add those memories to a bank of bittersweet thoughts that would have to last a lifetime. She loved Ethan. She always would. She'd never be with anyone else.

Callie had felt incredibly generous when she'd called him yesterday evening, offering to bring Luke by for a few hours today while she and her sisters shopped.

But LeeAnn had answered the confounded phone.

LeeAnn.

Still in his life.

After everything.

This needed to be settled.

First thing this morning, Callie had dug the divorce papers from her zippered luggage compartment. She'd also found her wedding ring. She'd slipped it on her finger for a brief moment, preferring the look of her hand so much more with it on.

But Josie had come from the shower just then, so

Callie had yanked it off and returned it to her luggage pocket.

When she'd loaded Luke's diaper bag for his outing this afternoon, she'd put the envelope containing the divorce papers right on top. If she handed Ethan the documents and suggested that they set up an appointment with his attorney, they would be forced to deal with the situation.

Perhaps they needed the wisdom of a judge to help make some of these decisions.

Josie made a sudden turn, causing the truck's wheels to squeal and pulling Callie's thoughts to the present. They were just a couple of minutes from Ethan's neighborhood.

"Are you sure you want to do this?" Josie asked.

"Yes. Absolutely," Callie said. "Ethan's off work today, so it makes sense for him to watch Luke. They'll have fun. They're really bonding."

Isabel must have heard the wobble in her voice, because she said, "That's a good thing, Callie. You know that."

Yes, it was. But it hurt because she felt left out. "Mmm-hmm."

"You'll work this out," Josie said. "You just need time."

Callie murmured another distracted *Mmm-hmm* and started gathering the diaper bag, the teddy bear Luke had dropped when he'd fallen asleep, and her wits.

When she noticed Ethan's empty driveway, she sighed in relief. At least LeeAnn wasn't here today.

After Josie had pulled into the drive, Callie released Luke's car seat from its bracket, deciding to carry him in while he was still asleep. She looped the diaper bag over her shoulder and waited for Isabel to get out of the two-door truck and push the seat forward. Then Callie slid across with Luke and his things, and got out.

After Isabel had returned to her seat and closed the

truck door, Callie leaned near the window to speak to her sisters. "I'm going to talk to Ethan a sec," she whispered. "Be right back."

She headed up the walkway and had only taken two steps before Ethan opened his front door, smiling widely.

What a great, great smile. Warm. Welcoming. Callie's heart lurched.

But when Ethan saw that the baby was asleep, he replaced his smile with an expression of determined caution.

Callie *so* preferred the other look.

Still, Ethan opened the storm door for her, then took the carrier and lowered it to the floor. "I appreciate your giving me this time with him."

Callie didn't answer. She leaned down to tuck the teddy bear in beside Luke's leg, then took a minute to fuss with his blanket. All she could think about was handing Ethan those divorce documents—even though she was reluctant to do so.

Now she wasn't avoiding divorce proceedings to protect her son from a divided life—that was inevitable, and she wanted only to make it as favorable to Luke as possible.

She resisted now only to protect herself. A less noble reason, certainly. And she had no choice. She had to proceed with the divorce. She needed to go home to Denver.

She stood up, glanced at Ethan, then peered down at the diaper bag suspended at her hip. She'd just unzipped it when she heard a screech of tires.

A Josie-taking-off-in-her-truck type of screech.

Callie and Ethan both stepped to the storm door to look out. Sure enough, Josie's silver Toyota was disappearing down the street. With Luke safely out of her truck, Josie had returned to her habitual recklessness. Didn't she realize that this was a residential street, where a child might dart from behind any bush?

And hadn't she forgotten something?

Someone?

Stepping outside, Callie ran into the yard and waved her arms. "Hey, stop!" she hollered.

Hadn't Josie heard her say that she'd be right back?

Was *she* coming right back?

What the heck was going on?

She asked this last question aloud to Ethan when he came out to stand beside her. Before he'd had a chance to offer his opinion, Luke began to cry.

They both rushed inside the house, but Ethan beat Callie to the carrier. He bent down to unbuckle the restraints, then lifted the baby into his arms.

Callie backed away, trying to avoid Luke's line of vision. Ethan needed a chance to calm him.

Ethan appeared relaxed, and he made all the right moves. He paced and bounced and soothed. Despite his efforts, Luke kept crying and asking for "Mum-mum."

Callie didn't think she'd ever been happier to hear her son crying for her. She stepped forward and took Luke in her arms, then sat on Ethan's sofa and hummed lullabies until the little boy grew quiet.

Then he leaned against Callie's chest, glancing around Ethan's living room with golden-brown eyes that were unusually wary.

Maybe Luke was more aware of the situation than Callie had realized. When her guy finally sat up in her arms, reaching for the toy bear he'd noticed in the carrier, Callie smiled.

Luke was fine. And she hadn't been easily replaced.

She handed Luke to Ethan, then bent down to grab the bear and hand it to her little boy.

"He'll be okay," she said. "He usually awakens in a great mood. Maybe he got scared when he woke up trapped in his seat, alone, and in a strange place."

"I'm sure," Ethan said, and turned his attention to Luke. He walked around his living room and made a running commentary on the teddy bear, the red-and-blue football-type jersey Luke wore today, and his plans for their afternoon together.

When Ethan rounded the corner beside the sofa, Luke looked down and pointed. "Dat-dat!" he said, bouncing excitedly.

Ethan chuckled, then wheeled out a colorful plastic push-and-ride toy from behind the sofa. "You found your train. Do you like it?" he asked, in an animated tone Callie had never heard him use before. Crouching down, he helped Luke stand next to the toy and grip its shiny green handle.

Ethan let go of him, and Luke stood for a moment opening and closing his fingers on the toy. He might have been content to do that for a while longer, but Ethan prompted him, "Now go, Lukey. Push the train!" He nudged the toy slowly forward.

The little boy's face crunched into a concentrated expression, and he wobbled forward. After two steps, his frown dissolved and he cackled as Ethan laughed.

They were fine. And Callie felt dismissed.

She didn't belong here, anyway. "Guess I'll go wait on the porch," she said.

Ethan glanced up. "Why?"

Because she felt too tied to both father and son, and watching them play from her spot outside the circle might break her heart.

"If she knows what's good for her, Josie will return

quickly," Callie said. "Maybe she just went around the block or to the corner store for a soda."

"Think so?" Ethan lifted a brow.

"Maybe Isabel will force her to come back," she said. Pulling the diaper bag off her arm, she remembered the envelope on top.

She'd meant to hand Ethan the divorce documents, suggest that they each contact a lawyer, then leave.

Heaven knew how long she'd be stranded here. She couldn't offer the papers and leave, and she didn't want to force the discussion in front of Luke. What if the little boy sensed the tension between his mother and this new man he liked so much?

She wouldn't hurt Luke that way, so she waited until a squeal caught Ethan's full attention, then yanked out the envelope. Quickly, she folded it in half twice lengthwise, then slid it into her jeans pocket and pulled her T-shirt down over it.

"Here are his things," she said, setting the diaper bag on an arm of the sofa. "I put in plenty of diapers and a box of teething biscuits for a snack. If he doesn't want those, there's also a jar of fruit and a spoon."

"Will he be hungry?"

"Possibly later, but he just ate lunch an hour ago."

Ethan glanced up. "All right. I think I can handle it."

"See you later."

"Okay," Ethan said. Then, "You can let yourself back in when you get hot."

She rolled her eyes, then walked outside and sat on his front porch step. She might have hidden the envelope in her purse, but she'd left her purse in Josie's truck.

Dammit.

What great ideas she'd had yesterday.

To come to Wichita with her sisters and shop for Isabel's new range—really, the last big task her sister had left to accomplish. To leave Luke at his dad's house, and continue to behave magnanimously. To drop off those papers and propel their lives forward, hoping to find a solution that would appease everyone.

Her ideas, every one.

Except she hadn't managed to accomplish a single one. What a waste of an afternoon.

ETHAN PLAYED with his son for twenty minutes, then picked him up and stepped out to his front porch. "Think she's had time to get around the block?" he asked Callie, who was sitting on the top step.

Callie glanced at him, then used her hand to shield her eyes from the sun's glare. "I don't guess they're returning any time soon."

"I don't guess so, either."

"If I had my purse, I'd call a cab and head home," she said, sighing as she returned her gaze to the street. "But then you'd miss your time with Luke."

There it was again—another display of that fair-mindedness.

Yesterday, LeeAnn had dropped by his house to return a jacket he'd left at her apartment. Even after he'd stated with certainty that their relationship was finished, she had stuck around to talk awhile.

He had told her how Callie was bringing Luke by all the time to give him opportunities to get acquainted with his little boy, and LeeAnn hadn't acted surprised.

She had warned him to watch out. Of course, Callie would be fair right now, she had said. Luke's custody arrangements would soon be determined by a judge, and she'd want to look good. She'd also want everyone concerned to forget about the whopping lie she'd kept going during the past two years.

Those insights had made sense. Wouldn't anyone try to present themselves in a good light? LeeAnn had certainly been on target about one thing: it was important that he maintain caution around Callie.

Last Saturday night, he might have thought himself ready for a reconciliation.

Last Sunday morning, Callie had proven that she still didn't trust men. Him, specifically.

It was hard to believe she couldn't know how much he loved her.

Had loved her.

He should distance himself. It would be smart to be wary, as LeeAnn had said. It might also be smart to leave Callie sitting on the porch, but he didn't intend to do so. They'd been close once. He couldn't forget that, even if Callie could. "Your sisters will come for you eventually, right?" he asked.

"Sure. This was just a ploy to get us talking again."

"We have been talking."

"Have we?" she asked, glancing back again. This time she didn't shield her eyes, and the sun lit them to a dazzling silver. He saw a lot of pain in those gorgeous depths. And he understood her question.

They might have talked, but not about anything significant.

Touché.

"Come on inside," he said, shifting Luke around to his other side so he could grab the door handle. "I can't have you sitting here glowering at every car that passes by. God only knows what my neighbors will think."

She sighed, scowling down the street again for a second, then she stood up. "If you have a book somewhere, I can find a quiet place to read."

"Why would you do that?"

"This is your time with him," she said, smiling at Luke. "I'd get in the way."

Another act of fairness.

Ethan pulled open the storm door and motioned for Callie to go in ahead of him. "Suit yourself. I have plenty of books in my office."

"Great. Where's your office?" She glanced toward the hall that led to his bedroom.

"The other way," he said. "The office and second bedroom are at the opposite end of the house." He put Luke near the new train toy and pointed the way for Callie. "Through that hallway, then right. Guess we spent most of our time in my bedroom the last time you were here."

Now why had he said that? It had revived memories he'd rather not recall. It hadn't been all that long since she'd been in his bedroom.

And in his arms and in his heart.

As Ethan watched her walk away, a new surge of desire for her surprised him. He couldn't be all that distant if he wanted her, could he?

The phone rang, saving him from contemplating his own question. It was Isabel, asking if Callie was still at his house. The question might seem silly, but Ethan knew Isabel pretty well. She was sharper than she let on. A determined Callie might have found any number of ways to get back to Augusta. Two years ago, she might have taken off on foot.

Why was Ethan so damn glad that she hadn't?

"Sure. She's still here," he said. "Just a moment."

Luke was playing with an activity console on the front

of the train, so Ethan left him in the living room for just a moment and went to his office.

Callie had already gotten comfortable in his leather office chair. She'd pulled an older mystery novel from his bookshelf and opened it to the first page.

He cleared his throat. "Izzy's on the phone for you," he said, pointing to the phone on his desk.

Leaving again, he lifted the receiver on the living room phone, waiting to hear Callie's voice before he hung up. Their conversation was none of his business.

Five minutes later, Luke glanced up from his play and said, "Mum-mum!"

Ethan realized that Callie had come to stand in the opening to the hallway. "Looks like I'll be here awhile," she said, shrugging. "Hope you don't mind."

"Where did they go?"

She sighed. "Appliance shopping, without me. Josie swears that we need time to work things out."

Right. Well, for Josie, life was uncomplicated in that way. She was honest with herself and everyone else about what she required. Except for a tendency to be blunt, she was nothing like her mother.

Callie had never been so easy. Marriage to her had been sometimes wonderful and sometimes painful.

Ethan hadn't responded to Callie's statement, but he must have looked skeptical, because she held his gaze for a moment, then said, "I know."

Sighing again, she entered the living room and pulled something from her back pocket. "Listen, I meant to leave these with you earlier. I didn't sign them."

Ethan took the envelope, which he recognized as the divorce papers.

"I'm sure we'll need different documents that indicate

the presence of a child in the marriage. And I'll have to hire my own lawyer, too."

Thrown by the mere mention of the divorce, Ethan scowled at Callie for a moment. Then he said, "We can call my attorney. I have his home number."

"We shouldn't use the same one, Ethan."

No, they shouldn't, Ethan decided. Initially, he'd thought that he and Callie could divorce amicably. But then, he was the same fool who'd believed that their marriage would last forever.

"We don't have to make any decisions today," he said. "But we need to find out if these papers are completely worthless."

"Don't contact him now," she insisted. "Not with Luke here. I want him to enjoy an afternoon with his dad. With you."

Ethan nodded.

"I should return to BioLabs soon, though, so we need to deal with this," she added. "Maybe tomorrow, one of us could contact a mediator."

Ethan merely nodded and watched Callie disappear into his office again. She was right. They shouldn't get into that particular discussion in front of Luke. In fact, they should vow to never argue in front of their son.

The little boy would have it hard enough, growing up in two different states with parents who had plenty of sizzle between them but not enough trust.

Callie had been taught to be wary of men, and he hadn't been able to convince her that males were no more or less disreputable than females.

And now he didn't trust her.

As if on cue, the little boy looked at him and said, "Mum-mum?"

"She's reading, Son. She's okay and so are you. I'm your daddy and I'm here for you this afternoon."

Luke squinted as if considering the many complexities of that statement, then he pulled himself up to stand next to the toy train and reached for Ethan.

Hurrying across the room, Ethan lifted his little boy into his arms, then walked to his kitchen table and set the envelope with a stack of mail.

Callie had been right not to sign the documents, too. A simple divorce wouldn't work, since they had a child.

Heaven knew what would work.

For now, Ethan intended to concentrate on his little boy. He glanced out the French doors. It was hot and sunny today, but two massive oak trees shaded the backyard. Ethan thought it might be nice to get Luke into the fresh air. To get himself outside, too, and perhaps forget about the confusing woman sitting in his office.

After retrieving the train, Ethan carried Luke outside and spent almost an hour watching the little boy play.

Luke sat on the train's seat, chuckling merrily while Ethan pushed it around in a dirt patch beneath one of the trees. When the child fell off, he didn't cry. He spent long minutes investigating the dirt. A butterfly flitted by, and he chased it across the grass on his hands and knees. Then Ethan held his hands and helped him walk all the way to the back gate, where he gripped the chain-link fence and watched a neighbor's cat slink through the alley.

After a time, Luke plopped onto his bottom again and looked mournful, as if he'd exhausted the whole outdoors. On closer examination, Ethan noticed that Luke's bottom eyelids were pink. He must be tired. Ethan picked him up and went inside, bouncing and humming all the way.

He wanted to learn to soothe Luke, but the baby soon started sobbing. Then squirming. And, finally, calling for his "Mum-mum."

Ethan poked his head into his office, where Callie had laid the book facedown on the desk. She must have restrained an impulse to rescue her baby. "Is he okay?" she asked.

"He's tired." Ethan crossed the room, and Luke quieted as soon as they drew near Callie.

"He slept in the car, but that wouldn't have been long enough," Callie said. She grinned when she saw a couple of dirt smears across the boy's cheek. Grabbing a tissue from Ethan's desk, she wiped them off. "You wore him out."

"Are you kidding? He wore me out."

She chuckled. "Do you have a place for him to sleep?" she asked. "The spare bedroom, maybe?"

"That room's empty. He can sleep in my bed."

She nodded. "Perfect."

Ethan headed for the bedroom, but when Luke cried out again he turned around. "I need your help with this."

"Okay." Her voice was bright, and…was that a smile?

"Why are you so happy all of a sudden?" he asked.

"No reason, really." When she was halfway out of the room, she added, "But it's nice to feel needed again."

In his bedroom, she said, "Just put him in the middle and stack pillows on the edges so he can't roll off."

But when Ethan put Luke down, the little boy cried.

"He doesn't know this room," Callie said. "You might have to *lie* with him until he goes to sleep."

"You haven't spoiled our little boy, have you?" Ethan asked, giving her a stern glance that was only half in jest.

Luke's cries got louder.

Ethan decided that now was not the time to try to *un-*

spoil the baby. He crawled onto the edge of the bed, lying face-to-face with Luke and patting the little boy's leg.

Luke quieted. His eyes drooped.

"Okay," Callie whispered. "He should be all right."

When she tried to tiptoe away, Luke's bottom lip stuck out. "Mum-mum?" he said, his eyes filling.

Callie chuckled, then turned right around. "Okay. Maybe I should stay and you should go."

Ethan slid off the bed so she could take his spot. She lay beside Luke, and the little boy put his chubby hand against her neck and sighed. Ethan backed toward the door.

Luke flopped over onto his tummy, lifted his little bottom high and pushed his arms up. After dropping his knees, he scrambled toward the edge of the bed. He made the funniest buzzing whine, sounding as if he was determined to catch up to his big new buddy.

"Guess that won't work, either," Callie said as she caught Luke in her arms.

Ethan returned to the side of the bed, gazing at mother and son. He shouldn't crawl in beside them. Callie's long hair was spread across the pillow and her gray eyes glowed with amusement.

LeeAnn would sure as hell tell him he shouldn't.

But Luke's brown eyes demanded the presence of both parents.

"It's all right, Ethan," Callie said softly. "We'll stay only until he goes to sleep. Nothing can happen with him right here between us."

That was how Ethan wound up in bed with Callie again, watching her pat their son's bottom and sing a medley of lullabies that he had long forgotten.

And that was how he forgot his intention to stay out of love with his soon-to-be ex-wife. Again.

So much for keeping an emotional distance.

When Callie stopped singing a couple of moments later, Ethan started to get up.

She shook her head. "Wait," she mouthed, pointing at the baby and making a sleeping motion by joining her palms and resting her head against them.

So he waited and tried not to stare. He felt oddly exposed, as if this was his first time seeing someone he cared about. Someone he had hurt.

Ethan shut his eyes.

Surely, that thought was confused. Callie had hurt *him.* She had withheld the truth about his son's identity.

Because you left her.

When the marriage was failing.

When she was struggling with a lot of problems that she needed to work out for herself.

And now he threatened to take the baby she'd wanted so desperately.

No matter how hard he tried, he couldn't stop wondering how much all of this was hurting her.

About how much *he* was hurting her.

Maybe the biggest mistake in resolving conflict, he decided at that moment, was in trying to decide exactly who the *good guys* and *bad guys* were.

Maybe everyone fell somewhere in the middle.

Chapter Twelve

"Hey, are you going to sleep, too?" Callie whispered.

When Ethan opened his eyes, she hitched her head toward the hallway. Luke was sleeping soundly, now. They could leave.

Slipping off her side of the bed, she stacked pillows around Luke to keep him from rolling off, then walked out.

Ethan followed her to his living room, where they stood eyeing each other.

"We can talk now," she said.

"Guess so." Ethan stuck his hands in his pockets.

"It's quiet in here."

"Yes, it is." Ethan nodded toward his seating area.

Callie sat on the sofa again and Ethan claimed one of the chairs across from her, and they sat silently, trading stares as if they were a blind-date couple meeting for the first time in a parent's living room. With the parent present. After they'd each taken a good look and decided they didn't like what they saw.

"Oh, for heaven's sake," she finally said. "We've known each other for too long to be this nervous about talking. We've always found things to talk about."

"Maybe. But we have bigger things to talk about now. And big decisions to make."

"Huge decisions." Callie shook her head. Then she made a vague, sweeping motion with her hand that she hoped would convey more than her words. "I'm sorry about all this."

Ethan nodded, as if he'd understood that her apology had been all-inclusive.

She hoped so.

Because she had meant about everything: The lie about Luke. The separation before that. Everything from their very first lover's spat two months after their wedding, to now.

She smiled sadly, remembering that first argument about tomatoes, of all things, and how to store and slice them. They'd each sulked for an entire day. Callie had recognized the stupidity of their argument, but she'd been frightened by their mutual anger.

She'd worried that the marriage was ending, even then. But after that day, Ethan had deferred to her knowledge about produce storage. She'd learned that he was the more knowledgeable cook.

And they'd made it eight more years.

Too bad things had gotten so complicated since then.

"I'm sorry, too," Ethan said quietly.

"For what?"

"Everything."

She smiled. "After last Saturday night, I had trouble figuring out how to tell you about Luke," she said. "I dreaded your reaction."

"I probably reacted worse than you expected."

Callie puffed out a breath and brushed her hair away from her face—summoning a bravery that came easier now that Ethan wasn't so aloof. "Not really. Yes, you did get angry," she said. "And I didn't want to face that, but your reaction was normal."

"I played my part in our problems," he said.

"I didn't mean to hurt you, Ethan," she said. "I knew you'd be a wonderful dad, but I couldn't face the idea of losing Luke. After he was born, the fierceness of my love for him surprised me."

"I know. I feel that way already."

She nodded. "I can tell."

He stared at her for a long moment. She wondered if he was thinking the same thing she was—that the path they'd taken in their marriage was so very far from their original intent.

"We've made a mess of things, haven't we?" he said, grinning.

That flash of a smile mesmerized her. Though brief, it had been incredibly warm and, most importantly, directed toward *her*.

His question had made her feel closer to him, too.

We've made a mess, he'd said.

Not you or I.

We.

As if they were a pair again.

She nodded. "Yes. An awful mess."

"Think it's fixable?" he asked, his brown eyes dark with questions.

Callie frowned, unsure about how to answer. Which mess? The problem of Luke's custody, the divorce that never happened, or their constantly changing relationship?

After a moment, she realized that she could answer his question the same way, however he'd meant it. She shook her head and said, "I don't know."

She didn't.

She didn't know how to divide their parenting so that it would be fair to both of them and to Luke.

She didn't know if she wanted a divorce at all, and yet she didn't know if they could get past their problems and make a success of their marriage.

She did know one thing, though. She desperately wanted to know Ethan's thoughts.

Did he want to try again?

Callie's eyes grew hot and heavy with tears, and that made her mad. She'd cried more since Ethan's departure than during her entire adult life. She'd cried about everything from her mom's lonely life to Luke's first baby tooth. Sometimes, she'd found herself crying over a newspaper cartoon.

When she felt a tear slip down her cheek, followed by another and finally a cascade, Callie swore under her breath. If she lost her composure, she certainly couldn't help Ethan make sense of things.

But Ethan moved across to sit on the sofa next to her, then looped an arm around her waist to pull her against his shoulder. "Hey, it's okay," he said. "We'll work it out."

Work what out? The problems of the divorce and Luke's custody?

Or the problems, period?

Ethan pulled his face far enough away to regard hers. He used his thumbs to wipe away the moisture, then he kissed the places he'd wiped.

He maneuvered his hands around to the small of her back and pulled her nearer, then he brought his mouth to hers. Gently, he kissed her. His mouth was closed, but soft.

Kissing was much easier than trying to talk. Ethan's pliant lips answered so many of her questions without the necessity of a single word.

When he kissed her, she sensed his caring. She knew he needed and wanted her. So she opened the kiss and let him know she felt the same.

Ethan deepened the intimacy more by teasing her tongue with a quick brush of his, then meeting it again with an urgent sexuality that had her gripping his shoulders and pressing closer.

She couldn't get near enough. They were side by side on the sofa, with legs and cushions and buttons in the way. Ethan must have recognized her frustration, because he slid an arm beneath her knees and another around her back, then he lifted her across his lap.

He was aroused.

Wonderfully aroused. Callie moaned, loving the feel of his hard length against her.

He kissed her again, but kept his hands at her thigh and back. Gentlemanly. As if he'd drawn a line between them that said this much was okay, but this much wasn't.

Immediately, Callie turned to straddle his lap, crossing that line. This desire between them might be wrong on some rational level, but it felt good and it was persistent.

In any case, they were still married.

Grabbing her blouse at the hem, Callie lifted it off and dropped it to the floor. Then, without taking her gaze from his, she unhooked her bra and tossed that down, too.

Let him see the evidence of *her* desire.

Let him feel it.

He groaned, then lifted his hands to her breasts. He fingered her taut nipples and claimed her lips again, thrilling her with deep, endless kisses that felt sensual and forgiving and right.

After a while, he shifted his hands to her hair and his lips to her neck. She'd always loved the way those tiny kisses sent shivers down her spine.

Once, she'd have exposed her neck for him, occupying

her hands by exploring his body. Today, she worried that he would stop.

Petting wasn't enough. She wanted to love him in the most meaningful way. "I want you inside me," she whispered.

"You're sure?"

"Oh, yes."

He let go of her, allowing her to scramble off his lap. She stood next to the sofa on shaky legs, glancing toward his windows to ensure they were curtained before she slipped off the rest of her clothes.

He followed her lead, managing to undress before she'd finished.

She didn't hesitate.

She flattened a palm against his chest, pushing him against the sofa cushion. After ridding herself of her panties, she straddled his lap again and looped her legs around his torso.

She wanted to see him, face-to-face in the afternoon light. As she eased his erection inside her, she gasped at the fullness of her body and heart, crying out at her intense feelings.

She didn't mind the tears this time. She wanted Ethan to see how much she needed him.

The quiet living room filled with sounds that couldn't be as loud as they sounded. The satisfying smack of kisses. Startled chuckles. Muffled moans and ragged breaths.

This was Callie's first time making love to Ethan since he'd learned the truth about their baby. She felt more vulnerable.

More aroused, too.

Now that he'd had time to adjust to the truth, some wall between them had crumbled. Honesty heightened their intimacy.

But this was also her first time making love to anyone with a baby in the house. If she and Ethan had stayed together, they'd have learned all the tricks that loving parents must know. They hadn't, so Callie worried that her son would awaken.

She wanted to be quiet, and she wanted to finish before they were interrupted.

Instead of closing her eyes, she watched the coupling of her body with Ethan's. She slid her hands along his flat, muscled tummy, reveling in the look and feel of their bodies, together.

Immediately, she climaxed.

She shuddered and closed her eyes, stilling her movements for a moment.

"Cal?"

Opening her eyes, she caught Ethan's questioning expression and nodded. "Don't worry, I'm not done," she murmured, beginning to move again.

Then she followed his pace, watching the strong man she loved achieve a shuddering satisfaction while her body found a deeper and more lingering response.

While baby Luke slept on.

"Man," Ethan said a moment later as he reclined against the sofa cushion and caught his breath. "It's hard to be quiet."

"I know."

"I think we might have set a time record, too."

She was glad to know they were thinking the same things. She leaned forward against Ethan's chest and listened to his heart find its normal rate.

Soon, they'd be able to put words to these actions. Maybe they could let all the bad history fall to the wayside, and concentrate on their most basic feelings for each other.

They might even be able to talk about it all before she left his house today.

Callie had every reason to believe so, until she heard another screech of tires. She peered through the curtains.

"That's Josie!" she exclaimed, pulling immediately away from Ethan to jump off the sofa and grab her panties.

He was up and off the sofa alongside her. He grabbed his clothes and half of hers, and had sprinted halfway to his bedroom before he remembered and announced, presumably to himself as well as her, "Luke's in there!"

So they ran to his office, each dressing on the way. He finished before she did, and as the doorbell rang he waved her into a second bathroom. "Get decent," he said. "I'll answer the door and tell them you're napping with Luke."

She nodded.

Moments later, she walked to his living room carrying the still-sleeping Luke and feeling about as composed as she could.

She hated what had just happened.

They had both felt compelled to run and hide.

But they were married. They had a right to have sex, whenever and wherever, until the day they were no longer married.

Of course, they'd want to be dressed for company, but she wished Ethan wasn't talking about Isabel's brand-new smooth-top range and pretending that Callie had just awakened from a nap.

She wanted to tell her sisters they should always call before they visited a married couple. She wanted Ethan's hair to be more mussed—when had he found time to comb it?—and she wanted him to look at her as he had on that sofa, and not as if she was merely the Blume sister who had once happened to be his wife.

She wanted to stay married to him.

She just wished she'd had time to find out if this afternoon had meant as much to him as it had to her.

AN HOUR AFTER Callie and her sisters had left with Luke, Ethan busied himself with grilling some steaks and portobello mushrooms for dinner. He didn't know what would happen with Callie, but he suspected that this afternoon had marked a step forward. Whatever else had happened between them, whatever their stupid reasons for letting go, they loved each other.

That was cause enough to celebrate.

Wonderful smells wafted from the grill, so Ethan tested the sizzling steaks by poking an index finger into the thickest part of the bigger one. It sprang back against his finger, hot and juicy but not too soft, so he grabbed his spatula and transferred both filets to the plate next to the mushrooms.

He'd always made two of whatever he was having—two chops, two burgers, two skewers of shrimp. Sometimes LeeAnn or a buddy showed up to have dinner with him. Sometimes he stuck the extra in the fridge for leftovers. He hadn't realized it at the time, but he must have always had Callie in mind.

He'd never stopped thinking about her. Not for a meal, not for another woman. Not for a moment.

Deciding to forego his usual habit of eating in front of a TV news program when he was alone, Ethan carried the steaks inside to his kitchen table. Dropping his basketball to the floor and a box of stale chocolates into the trash, he plunked his plate in the cleared spot. Then he scrounged a linen napkin and utensils and set those on the table before putting crushed ice, filtered water and a lemon slice in his glass.

Callie had always insisted that they eat meals with the same level of civility that they would adopt in a restaurant. She'd also preferred a regular time for eating, claiming that that was the way of families. She'd wanted to raise their child in a household containing a wealth of such traditions.

After he'd left, Ethan had immediately changed his habits. In fact, he'd done everything in a manner that would have chafed at Callie's nerves. He'd left his newspapers lying around on the table and countertops, he'd eaten on the run and he'd washed his black socks with his white T-shirts whenever it suited him.

Now he recognized the childishness of his rebellion.

Ethan cut off a piece of steak and lifted it to his mouth, savoring it even while he wished that Callie were here to share the other. He could have asked her to stay this evening. He'd wanted to, until her sisters had arrived to scramble the situation.

After ushering Isabel and Josie inside, he'd had to concentrate hard to make small talk. Ten minutes later, Callie had appeared with their sleeping boy and whispered that if they got on the road to Augusta he'd stay asleep.

The Blume sisters had all tiptoed out.

Since he didn't know what Callie was telling her sisters about their changing relationship, Ethan hadn't wanted to insist on a more satisfying goodbye. He thought he'd seen an apology in Callie's expression, but he didn't know the reason for her regret—her departure at such a lousy time, or their wild afternoon together.

As Ethan ate a mushroom, he noticed the envelope Callie had given him, lying beside him on the table. Grimacing, he put down his fork and slid the divorce documents off the stack of mail.

After studying the front of the envelope for a moment, he got up to toss the confounded thing in the trash without opening it. It was obsolete, as Callie had pointed out. No need to keep it lying around.

Again, he wished she were here so they could talk about things. This afternoon might have proven their stubborn desire for each other, but they still had so much else to resolve.

He was still thinking about Callie after he'd finished the steak, washed the dishes and put away the junk on the kitchen table, so he decided to phone her. He'd insist that they get together again soon. Tomorrow, he determined as he dialed.

She could tell her sisters she was bringing Luke to see him in the afternoon. Or, better yet, she could arrive in the morning. They could spend the entire day together and talk in between sessions of entertaining Luke.

Or…what about tonight?

What about telling her sisters that she loved her husband and intended to move her things out to his house? That she needed Luke to live with both parents, as God had no doubt intended?

"Hullo?" The voice on the line sounded very much like Callie's, but Ethan identified Izzy's slightly higher pitch.

"Hi, Izzy. This is Ethan. Is she there?"

A heavy sigh. "Yes, but she's really busy."

Isabel sounded rushed herself, and also reluctant. Ethan wondered why Callie's sister was screening her telephone calls.

He remembered the afternoon months ago when Isabel had met him at the front door of her flood-ravaged house, protecting her sister by trying to keep him outside.

Now he knew why.

Callie had been hiding Luke from him that day. Perhaps she'd been worried about him recognizing his own son. She hadn't simply been upset about seeing him again. And she hadn't been avoiding a divorce because she'd wanted to stay married to him.

But why would she try to evade him now? Could this afternoon have scared her? She'd initiated the lovemaking. Hell, she'd practically demanded it. Perhaps the intensity of the experience had frightened her.

Ethan squelched his worry, choosing to assume that Isabel's behavior stemmed from ignorance about their afternoon together. "Tell Callie it's me," he said, adopting a tone of confidence. "She'll talk to me."

"All right."

Ethan heard a silence as Isabel stepped away from the phone, then voices filled the void. He couldn't make out words until Josie hollered something about packing Luke's clean jammies.

"Hello?" Callie said a moment later.

"Hi, it's me."

"Ethan! Good heavens!"

"We need to talk," he said quickly, before she could think of reasons to resist. "I thought we might get together tomorrow to —"

"I can't."

Can't wasn't a word the old Callie had used often. Ethan wondered what had happened. He sat in a chair at the kitchen table and glanced at the spot where the divorce papers had been. "Why not?" he asked.

Callie let out a forceful sigh. "When we got to Josie's apartment a while ago, Stan from BioLabs had left a message on her answering machine," she said. "Patty and Stan had a huge argument, and she walked off the job. Stan's been at the lab all weekend and can't find some of the research files. I have to return to straighten a few things out."

She was returning to Colorado now, after this afternoon?

"You must realize that we need to talk first," he said. "I can take tomorrow off work and we can—"

"Ethan!"

"Yes?"

"I'm leaving tonight."

Oh, no. She couldn't go back and get involved with that infernal job again. She'd get absorbed in her work, and Ethan might have to send divorce papers in the mail.

He might have to live five hundred miles from the woman he loved, and from the son he'd only recently met.

That couldn't happen. Even if he and Callie couldn't fix their damaged relationship, he intended to be a hands-on father. They had to find a way to share time with their little boy.

"Callie, that place can survive without you," he said. "You may be a brilliant scientist, but they'd replace you if you left."

"That's just it, Ethan," she said. "This project is mine. I won the grant. If I don't retrieve the lost data now, the lab could lose their funding for this piece of research."

Her argument was old, and it didn't work for Ethan now any more than it ever had. Her work might be vital, but she couldn't exist for that research. Even if she didn't know it, she needed the support of someone other than her co-workers.

He wanted to believe that she needed him.

At least now, Ethan had an extra argument for his side. "Isn't Luke's future just as important—more important— than that job, Cal?"

Aren't I?

"Yes, of course. I'm not planning to stay—not this trip." She paused, then added softly, "I know we have important things to talk about."

Ethan wanted to trust her, but he'd learned the truth about Luke's identity only a week ago. If LeeAnn hadn't been a more astute observer than Ethan, he might have never known.

Would Callie have told him? He asked himself that question constantly. He wanted to believe her claims, but circumstances made that difficult.

"It's almost five-thirty, Cal. When are you leaving?"

"I have a seven-fifteen flight out of Wichita. I'm almost packed. After I feed Luke his dinner, I'm leaving for the airport."

LeeAnn might be right about Callie's less-than-honorable motives. If he hadn't telephoned Callie tonight, she might not have told him she was leaving for Denver.

She'd been surprised to hear from him, hadn't she? Evidently, she'd been planning to catch that flight without telling him she was going.

A sense of hopelessness darkened Ethan's thoughts. He wanted to take Callie at her word, but how could he allow her to take his son away? How could he take the risk of losing both of them again?

Ethan had an idea. "You're returning soon?" he asked. "Within days?"

"Probably."

"Then leave Luke with me. I'll feed him dinner tonight. You concentrate on packing."

"What?"

"I'm his dad. Leave him here."

Callie remained silent for a long while. "Oh, Ethan, I

don't know," she finally said. "I don't want to make this decision on impulse."

"He's my son, too, Cal."

She sighed. "Except for a couple of short play dates, you haven't been responsible for Luke on your own. Do you even know how to feed him? Would you be able to console him if he cried for days on end?"

"He'd do that?" Ethan asked.

"He has before."

"Then I'd handle it."

To Ethan's mind, Callie's brief consideration of his idea held an aura of faith. He met it with confidence. "I've watched you feed him, and I know to keep my eye on him in the tub. I'll contact you if I have questions," he promised. "And if I can't get you, I'll telephone Isabel."

Callie didn't say a word.

"Unpack his things and put them in a separate suitcase or a paper sack," he said. "Were you planning to take that portable crib?"

"No. Luke has a big crib at home."

"Toss it in your trunk and bring it here."

"Ethaa-nn!"

"My house is on your way to the airport," he said. "Swing by here and I'll follow you, then you can list instructions while you're waiting to board. But you'd better get moving."

"Don't you have to work?" she asked. "What will you do with him then? And don't you have to be on call for emergencies?"

He hadn't thought that far ahead. "Where does he go while you work?" he asked.

"The lab has an in-house day care where I can visit him over my lunch break. They tell me if he even fusses."

But those day care workers were only employees. No

one could look out for his son as conscientiously as he would. Callie would recognize that. "I'll take time off work. I'll protect that little boy with my life. You know I will."

She hesitated, then let out a sigh. "Yes, I do. He'll be fine with you."

"Then it's settled," Ethan said, satisfied with this mutual decision that was unquestionably another step forward. He looked forward to spending the next few long, fun-filled days with his son.

Chapter Thirteen

By the next afternoon, Ethan had decided that the next few days would certainly be long, but he wasn't sure he could pull off the *fun-filled* part. He also wondered about his sanity. On a full-time basis, babies were exhausting.

He'd handled meals and bath times all right. Luke liked to eat and he loved to play in the bathtub, so those tasks hadn't been impossible to manage.

Sleep times were another story. Last night, Ethan had paced the floor with Luke in his arms, trying to get the very tired, very fussy child to relax. He'd started trying as soon as he and Luke had returned from the airport, and he'd still been trying shortly after ten o'clock, when Callie had telephoned from her Denver townhome to tell him that she'd made it in all right.

He'd finally crashed on the sofa with Luke on his chest, and he'd awakened a few hours later when the kid had drooled on his neck and earlobe.

He couldn't do that again.

Neither one of them had gotten enough sleep. Their crankiness had made the morning incredibly wearing.

The afternoon was worse. Right now, Ethan was in his second hour of trying to get the kid to nap, and he had ignored several urges to telephone Callie for advice. He didn't want her to worry. He wanted her to fix the lab problems and rush back to Kansas.

He could handle his son.

He *could.*

Luke simply needed to adjust to a slight change in routine.

Ethan had tried leaving the baby in the portable crib a while ago, but he'd found it impossible to ignore those mournful cries for "Mum-mum." He had then lain in his own bed beside Luke, but even that hadn't worked.

Remembering that Callie had mentioned Luke sleeping in the car, Ethan loaded the boy in his car seat and started driving.

The kid obviously missed his mother.

So did Ethan, and not just because he hadn't had more than four hours' sleep last night.

He missed *her.*

As soon as she returned from Denver, Ethan wanted to get Isabel to babysit Luke for as long as necessary, and he wanted to sit with Callie and talk this through. Perhaps they should sit in Isabel's house, where they wouldn't be tempted to kiss.

He'd start by talking about Denver. He'd mention the importance of her job, then point out that even leaders of countries didn't hold their positions forever. He'd also ask if she was certain she could live that far from her sisters again. And from him.

Or maybe he wouldn't ask that question. She hadn't taken it well, before. If she asked, he would even return to Denver to try again. All Ethan really wanted to know was if Callie saw any hope for them, as a couple. Could they possibly mend their relationship?

The drive worked. Luke fell asleep before Ethan had made it as far as east Wichita. He didn't want to risk waking the baby, so he continued on to Augusta, passing by Josie's apartment and finally Isabel's house.

The inspector's placard had been removed. Isabel had put new lace curtains on her front window, and they were open. Under different circumstances, Ethan might have stopped by to say hello, but he wanted his son to have a long nap.

He circled back round to Wichita, then continued on the highway in the opposite direction. Tonight, he'd learn to put the kid in his crib to fall asleep on his own. By the time Callie returned, he'd have sleep times conquered.

He *would*.

Luke didn't awaken until an hour and a half later, when his too-weary father had pulled into a fast-food drive-through for a monster-size cup of coffee.

The little boy had awakened in a good mood, so Ethan stopped by a toy store on the way home. Maybe he could exhaust the kid and make his daunting evening project a little easier.

Seven hours later, Ethan walked the floor with Luke again and tried to ignore the third ring of his doorbell. He was in no mood for a visitor, and Luke was finally relaxing. He might be going to sleep.

Luke bucked his head back and shoved a fist across his pink-lidded eyes. "No-no-no," he said crankily, his chin dripping with drool and tears.

Obviously, the baby wasn't sleeping.

Ethan might as well answer the confounded door. He strode across the space and yanked it open to scowl at Lee-Ann, who had paired her standard hat and boots with a crisp white suit. "Not a good time," he barked, rounding immediately into the living room again. "Enter at your own risk."

"Mum-mum-mumm," Luke said with a pout, butting his wet face against Ethan's shoulder.

"What happened?" LeeAnn asked, staring at both of them.

"Nothing," Ethan said, shrugging. "It's bedtime."

When Luke's whimpers grew louder, Ethan started bouncing and pacing until the weary little guy quieted again.

"Where's his mother?" LeeAnn asked.

"Callie's gone to Denver for a few days."

LeeAnn frowned. "Well. That's surprising, isn't it? She just left the kid with you? I took her to be more devoted than that."

"I talked her into leaving him with me," he said. "Listen, LeeAnn, you should just go. As I told you the other day, I'm in no position to date."

She glanced at Luke, who was temporarily quiet but not at all asleep, then returned her gaze to him. "Did I suggest otherwise?"

She hadn't suggested it, but since she was still coming around, he figured she wanted something. He figured she was waiting around for the big breakup.

"Even if Callie and I don't work out our problems," he said, "I'm going to concentrate on being a dad for a while."

"I do have a thought about that," she said, stepping forward to peer closely at Luke.

"What is it?" he asked.

She smiled. Shrugged. "Maybe he's not yours."

Ethan scowled. "Oh, come on. You said yourself that he has my hair and eyes. He laughs the same way I do. He even has my toes."

She glanced at Luke's feet. "Could be a coincidence. And Callie could have slept with another man with dark brown hair, light brown eyes and dimples."

He chuckled. "LeeAnn, what are you doing?"

"About what?" She batted her eyelashes.

"Why are you here? We were never that involved. Why not just find a guy who can devote himself to you?"

"Oh, sure. I will," she said with a sulky expression that rivaled Luke's. "I'm just helping you through a rough time. You're a nice guy, and I'd hate to see you hurt."

"Is that it?" he asked quietly. "Or is it that this is the first time in a while you haven't won? You told me once that you were valedictorian and prom queen at your high school, and that every guy you've set your sights on has dated you until you broke things off."

"So?"

"So, maybe you aren't letting go because for the first time, you aren't in control."

She hesitated, as if truly considering his suggestion, but then she snickered and shook her head. "Whatever. Todd's been taking me out, and he's really sweet," she said. "So no problem. I'd still advise you to get a paternity test before you make any major decisions."

"Dat!" Luke mumbled, wiggling in Ethan's arms.

Ethan didn't even look to see what his son wanted. Something about this part of the conversation disturbed him, and he'd pursue it until he knew why. Gently, he put his son on the floor and gazed at LeeAnn.

"My paternity is not in question," he told her.

"Why not? The day I came to Augusta, I watched Callie's sisters. They were trying to give her time alone with you. They might all be plotting to win you back."

"Think so?"

LeeAnn lifted a brow. "A lot of women sleep with look-alikes of their exes," she said. "I have. So have some of my girlfriends. Callie isn't as different as you think."

Ethan thought about that.

No. LeeAnn was wrong. Callie was every bit as different as he thought, and in the best of ways. She wouldn't have slept with another man, look-alike or not.

He knew that.

Then the ton of bricks hit him.

The problems that had been driving him mad became solvable.

The mistakes, on both sides, forgivable.

"Thank you," he said, stepping forward to kiss LeeAnn on the cheek before he took her elbow and led her toward the door. "You've just done me a favor."

"What did I do?" LeeAnn asked. When she realized he was guiding her through the door, she changed the question. "What are you doing?"

"You helped me realize something," he said when he let her go on his front porch. "And I intend to do whatever it takes to convince Callie that we should stay married."

"Why?"

"I don't need to tell you why," he said. "I appreciate the time we've spent together, LeeAnn. But I love Callie and always will. Sorry. I wish you well."

Ethan watched her leave, grateful that her walk was still confident. He couldn't have hurt her too much.

He and LeeAnn might have enjoyed each other's company for a time, but they had never been destined for more than a casual dating relationship. Perhaps he'd needed to reembrace the idea of loving someone.

LeeAnn would land on her feet. She'd probably have a

hot date with a mandolin player within an hour. And except for those Saturday-night soirees with Callie, Ethan's days of dating were finished.

He hoped.

God. He hoped.

After closing the door, he crossed the living room to retrieve his little boy from beneath the red-and-yellow plastic fort he'd bought this afternoon. It was probably a mistake, trying to get the kid to sleep with that big, colorful toy within his sight.

Pulling Luke into a hug, Ethan walked down the hall and peered into the second bedroom—now Luke's room.

No. That room also had a few too many bright, plastic things. What had Ethan been thinking?

Deciding the hallway was the safest best, Ethan paced there. He relaxed more, even if Luke didn't. After a time, the baby let out a huge sigh and drooped in Ethan's arms. He'd gone to sleep.

Carrying the baby to the crib, Ethan laid him down and left the room. He wished he could talk to Callie now, but he had to wait. A wise man didn't declare his affections over the phone.

Then Ethan walked around his quiet house, picking up toys and thinking. The next few days would be fun. He enjoyed his son's company immensely, and they could help each other pass the time until the woman they loved called to say she was returning.

As CALLIE FELT the airplane make its descent, she toyed with her wedding band. She'd returned it to her finger soon after she'd arrived at the townhome and located it in her luggage. She'd worn it ever since.

A sudden jolt indicated that the wheels of the plane had

made contact with the ground, then Callie felt a moment of lift and another bump before the rapid slowing.

She was ready to be home.

Was Kansas home?

Yes. Although Callie's specific place of residence was still in question. As the plane taxied toward the terminal, she glanced at the ring again. It belonged on her hand. She wouldn't take it off again until her divorce was final.

If her divorce became final.

She'd managed to straighten out the mess at BioLabs within four days, and she'd been surprised at the actual scope of the problems. Instead of spending her time locating research documents, she'd soothed hurt feelings. Patty and Stan had fallen into a relationship and had a serious quarrel, so Patty had walked off the job, inadvertently taking the files when she'd cleaned out her desk.

Callie found it amusing that she had left her own love life in turmoil to go settle another couple's romantic upset. Patty and Stan had just needed time to work things out. The files had been restored and so had Patty. She and Stan were now engaged, and the entire lab staff had expressed confidence that they could carry on with the research trials for as long as necessary.

That would be forever.

Callie had offered to supervise the project long-distance, but she'd given her notice. Her life was in Kansas.

When the seat belt light went off, Callie jumped up and grabbed her luggage from the overhead bin. She proceeded down the aisle as fast as the line of passengers allowed, then hastened into the concourse.

She knew now what she needed to do.

She'd tell Ethan everything. That she'd felt abandoned by him, and she'd made foolish decisions. She'd admit her share of the blame for their problems, from their very first lovers' tiff to the more weighty troubles of today.

She'd learned so much, after he'd left and since she'd been in Kansas.

She'd ask for another chance.

And another, if necessary.

And another, until their marriage came to a natural end when, hopefully, they were both very old.

As Callie strode through the terminal, she saw the handsome, dark-haired man standing in the hallway near the gift shop. He crouched near a stroller to point at her and speak to the little boy who wore the same dimpled grin he did.

Man, it was good to see them.

Callie broke into a jog. She could be about to make a huge fool of herself right now.

Ethan's eyes were lit, and Luke opened and closed his fist in the cutest wave Callie had ever seen.

"Hey!" she said softly as she approached. After Ethan had unbuckled Luke's restraint and taken Callie's bag, she lifted her little boy into her arms. "I missed you," she murmured, ostensibly to the child.

But her gaze rested on Ethan.

Ethan began to push the empty stroller toward the exit. "We're glad you're home," he said just as cryptically.

"Things went okay?" she asked.

"You know how things went. We talked every day."

"On the phone. But we can say more face-to-face," she pointed out. "Are you okay? I know Luke doesn't go to sleep easily when he's in unusual surroundings."

"We adapted," Ethan said, looking across her shoulder at Luke. "I think we came to a few understandings. Naps and bedtimes are not optional, but baths and playtimes can be creative."

She smiled back. "Good."

"You're acting pretty happy," he said. "You think your work problems are settled?"

"They're fine. I'll tell you about it later." Callie stopped walking and tugged on Ethan's shirtsleeve. "Wait a minute," she said, sighing. "Can I have a hug?"

He answered with a solid hug that made Luke chuckle, and followed that with a firm but chaste kiss that caused the little boy to squeal with glee.

Ethan let go, his eyes amused. "Will that do?"

"It will." As they resumed their walk, they didn't speak again. Callie had so much to say, but she wanted the time and setting to be perfect.

On the drive to his house, Ethan told her a few tales about Luke's morning, and when Callie walked into his living room moments later, she laughed.

The room contained a large, colorful play set, as well as the train. "Guess you went shopping," she said.

"We sure did," Ethan said. "Come look at what we put in the second bedroom."

Callie followed Ethan across the living room and rounded the corner as he opened the door. The once-empty space now held a small, red-framed toddler bed and a lightweight tent that contained hundreds of colorful plastic balls.

She put Luke down, expecting him to walk a few steps before he dropped into a crawl, but the little boy wobbled all the way to the ball pit.

She gasped. "Ethan, when did he start walking that far on his own?"

Ethan shook his head. "This is the first time I've seen

him," he said. "But then I didn't put him down much this weekend."

Callie chuckled. "Now who's spoiling him?"

"Not too much, I hope," Ethan said as he watched Luke. Then he returned his attention to Callie and moved forward. "Our son is busy."

"He is."

Ethan stopped just a few inches away from her. "Then this is a good time to talk."

Callie gazed at him. That gleam in his eyes suggested all kinds of wonderful things that had little to do with talking, so she was slightly surprised when he didn't lean in to kiss her.

"I didn't tell you everything over the phone," he said. "I had a visitor a couple of days ago."

She shook her head. "Who?"

"LeeAnn."

Callie crammed her eyes shut, then reopened one to peer worriedly at him. "You're still seeing her?"

"I stopped *seeing* her a while ago, after you and I got involved again." He shrugged. "She kept dropping by."

"I don't blame her for hanging on," Callie said. But her hope built in such a rush that her eyes teared.

"She's very competitive," he said. "But she and I were never meant to be together."

"You weren't?"

"No. I was glad she came by, though," Ethan said. "Something she said made things so much clearer for me."

"What was that?"

He pulled Callie into his embrace and spoke low in her ear. "She tried to put doubts in my head about my biological connection to Luke."

Callie shook her head. "Oh, but you know you're his

dad! Even if I had slept with another guy, which I didn't, I couldn't have gotten pregnant that way."

"I know," Ethan murmured. "I would have known even if you could get pregnant naturally. As long as you were married to me, you wouldn't sleep with some other guy."

"No."

"I also realized that I've been fooling myself," he said, his voice unsteady now. "I do trust you. And it must have taken an incredible amount of faith for you to leave Luke here with me these past few days."

She smiled.

"You knew I'd have some struggles with him, didn't you? With sleep times? With the relentless motion of a toddler?"

She nodded. "I did know, but I trusted that you'd survive and handle yourself well."

"I think we've both grown up some," he said. "Don't you?"

"Dat-dat-dat!" Luke said.

Both Callie and Ethan looked toward their son, who was tossing balls out of the tent enclosure.

"Do you mind that he's not your biological child?" Ethan asked.

"Of course not. I love the fact that he takes after you, but he's the child of my heart. That's all that matters."

"I knew you'd say that," Ethan said, tugging her forward to kiss her thoroughly. "I love you, Callie Taylor," he said after a while. "I always did. I was a fool to leave."

"I pushed you away. I think I might have been testing you, trying to prove my mother wrong," she said. Sighing, she shook her head. "Or right. I don't even know which, but I do know I wasn't fair to you."

When she lifted her left hand to show him her ring, he smiled. "You're wearing it?" he asked.

"I am."

"Stay right there."

He dashed down the hallway and returned a moment later with a gold band flashing brightly on his hand. After they'd admired their rings for a moment, he pulled her very close again and said, "Calliope Sloane Taylor, will you *stay* married to me?"

She smiled. "I will."

He kissed her for a good while. "Good," he said then. "Because I've contacted my old boss in Denver to see if they have any detective openings on their squad. We can start packing today."

Oh, no!

"Why?" Callie asked.

"Your research is there, and it is important. Cancer patients of the world need your brain in their corner." He looped one arm around her waist, used the other hand to grab hers and twirled her into the hallway.

"Why didn't we ever dance?" he asked.

"I don't know."

"Let's take lessons."

"Mmm. Sounds nice. A parents' night out."

After a few moments of twirling in the hallway with her handsome guy, Callie decided the lessons would be fun, but hardly necessary. They did fine.

"I don't need you to move to Denver for me, Ethan," she murmured against his ear.

He leaned back to peer into her eyes. "But I can work anywhere."

"So can I."

He stopped dancing. "What?"

"I had a few revelations during my time away, too," she said. "For one thing, I realized that my job is just a job. I can do the research in affiliation with one of Wichita's hospitals, or I can set up my own facility."

"You think so?"

"I don't think women with ovarian cancer would mind if every scientist in the country worked on finding a cure, do you?"

He shook his head, then pulled her into an embrace again and swayed to the sounds of a quiet house.

Callie glanced at Luke over Ethan's shoulder. The little boy had squatted down next to his ball pit, grasping at balls with both hands. Still busy.

Wrapping her arms tighter around Ethan's neck, Callie moved her face close to his. "Did I tell you that I adore your house?" she asked, keeping her mouth just a breath away from his. "The neighborhood, too. And this place is within driving distance of my sisters without being too near."

"I'm glad you like it," he said in a low voice.

"Luke likes this playground of a room," she added as they continued to dance very slowly, "and your bed is playground enough for me." She stopped moving. "Would you mind sharing this house with a wife and little boy?"

He answered with a chuckle, then another kiss. This one wasn't chaste or short or gentlemanly. He opened his mouth and let her feel his ardor.

Callie crammed her hands in Ethan's thick hair and made sure he didn't end the kiss too soon. She had just touched her tongue to her husband's when she felt a sudden, soft strike against her bottom, then her shoulder.

"Hey!" Ethan said, glancing sideways and down.

The little culprit stood in the doorway, cackling at them. Then he wobbled past them to retrieve one of the balls and throw it again.

They'd have to correct him soon. He'd need to know that he couldn't throw balls at people for sport. Well, at least not until he was old enough for dodgeball games at school.

For now, Callie laughed. She lifted her little boy into her arms, allowing him to join her within the embrace of the man they would each love for the rest of their lives.

Welcome to the world of American Romance!
Turn the page for excerpts from our
November 2005 titles.
CINDERELLA CHRISTMAS by Shelley Galloway
BREAKFAST WITH SANTA by Pamela Browning
HOLIDAY HOMECOMING by Mary Anne Wilson
Also, watch for a new anthology,
CHRISTMAS, TEXAS STYLE,
which features three fun and warmhearted
holiday stories by three of your favorite
American Romance authors,
Tina Leonard, Leah Vale and Linda Warren.
Let these stories show you what it's like to celebrate
Christmas down on the ranch.
We hope you'll enjoy every one of these books!

We're thrilled to introduce a brand-new author to American Romance! Prepare yourself to be pulled in by Shelley Galloway's characters, who you'll just like.
CINDERELLA CHRISTMAS is a charming tale of a woman whose need for a particular pair of shoes starts a chain of events worthy not only of a Cinderella story, but of a fairy tale touched with the magic of Christmas.

Oh, the shoes were on sale now. The beautiful shoes with the three gold straps, the four-inch heel and not much else. The shoes that would show off a professional pedicure and the fine arch of her foot, and would set off an ivory lace gown to perfection.

Of course, to pull off an outfit like that, she would need to have the right kind of jewelry, Brooke Anne thought as she stared at the display through the high-class shop window. Nothing too bold…perhaps a simple diamond tennis bracelet and one-carat studs? Yes, that would lend an air of sophistication. Not too dramatic, but enough to let the outfit speak for itself. Elegance. Refinement. Money.

Hmm. And an elaborate updo for her hair. Something extravagant, to set off her gray eyes and high cheekbones. Something to give herself the illusion of height she so desperately needed. It was hard to look statuesque when you were five-foot-two.

But none of that would matter when she stepped out on the dance floor. Her date would hold her tightly and twirl her around and around. She would balance on the pad of her foot as they maneuvered carefully around the floor. She would put all those dancing lessons to good use, and her date would be impressed that she could waltz with ease. They would glide through the motions, twirling, dipping, stepping together. Other dancers would stay out of their way.

No, no one would be in the way…they would have already moved aside to watch the incredible display of footwork, the vision of two bodies in perfect harmony, moving in step, gliding in precise motion. They would stare at the striking woman, wearing the most beautiful, decadent shoes…shoes that would probably only last one evening, they were so fragile.

She would look like a modern-day Mona Lisa—with blond hair and gray eyes, though. And short. She would be a short Mona Lisa. But, still graceful.

But that wouldn't matter, because she would have on the most spectacular shoes that she'd ever seen. She'd feel like…*magic.*

"May I help you?"

Brooke Anne simply stared at the slim, elegant salesman who appeared beside her. "Pardon?"

He pursed his lips, then spoke again. "Miss, do you need any help? I noticed that you've been looking in the window for a few minutes."

"No…thanks."

With a twinge of humor, Brooke Anne glanced in the window again, this time to catch the reflection staring back at her. Here she was, devoid of makeup, her hair pulled back in a hurried ponytail, dressed in old jeans and a sweatshirt that was emblazoned with Jovial Janitor Service. And her shoes…she was wearing old tennis shoes.

Pamela Browning has eaten breakfast with Santa.
It was a pancake breakfast fund-raiser for charity,
exactly like the one in her book,
and she attended dressed as Big Bird.
She thought she'd be able to relax with a big plate of
pancakes after leading the kids in songs from
Sesame Street, *but some of the more*
thoughtful children had prepared her a
plate of—you guessed it—birdseed.
When she's not dressing as an eight-foot-tall bird,
Pam spends her time canoeing, taking
Latin-dance lessons and, lately,
rebuilding her hurricane-damaged house.

Bah, humbug!

The Santa suit was too short.

Tom Collyer stared in dismay at his wrists, protruding from the fur-trimmed red plush sleeves. He'd get Leanne for this someday. There was a limit to how much a big brother should do for a sister.

The pancake breakfast was the Bigbee County, Texas, event of the year for little kids, and when Leanne had asked him to participate in this year's fund-raiser for the Homemakers' Club, he hadn't taken her seriously. He was newly home from his stint in the Marine Corps, and he hadn't yet adjusted his thinking back to Texas Hill Country standards. But his brother-in-law, Leanne's husband, had come down with an untimely case of the flu, and Tom had been roped into the Santa gig.

He peered out of the closet at the one hundred kids running around the Farish Township volunteer fire department headquarters, which was where they held these blamed breakfasts every year. One of the boys was hammering another boy's head against the floor, and his mother was trying to pry them apart. A little girl with long auburn curls stood wailing in a corner.

Leanne jumped onto a low bench and clapped her hands. "Children, guess what? It's time to tell Santa Claus what you want for Christmas! Have you all been good this year?"

"Yes!" the kids shouted, except for one boy in a blue velvet suit, who screamed, "No!" A nearby Santa's helper tried to shush him, but he merely screamed "No!" again. Tom did a double take. The helper, who resembled the boy so closely that she must be his mother, had long, gleaming wheat-blond hair. It swung over her cheeks when she bent to talk to the child. Tom let his gaze travel downward, and took in the high firm breasts under a clinging white sweater, the narrow waist and gently rounded hips. He was craning his neck for a better assessment of those attributes when a loudspeaker began playing "Jingle Bells." That was his cue.

After pulling his pants down to cover his ankles and plumping his pillow-enhanced stomach to better hide his rangy frame, he drew a deep breath and strode from the closet.

"Ho-ho-ho!" he said, making his deep voice even deeper. "Merry Christmas!" As directed, he headed for the elaborate throne on the platform at one end of the room.

"Santa, Santa," cried several kids.

"Okay, boys and girls, remember that you're supposed to sit at the tables and eat your breakfast," Leanne instructed. "Santa's helper elves will come to each table in turn to take you to Santa Claus. Remember to smile! An elf will take your picture when you're sitting on Santa's knee."

Tom brushed away a strand of fluffy white wig hair that was tickling his face. "Ho-ho-ho!" he boomed again in his deep faux-Santa Claus voice as he eased his unaccustomed bulk down on the throne and ceremoniously drew the first kid onto his lap. "What do you want for Christmas, little girl?"

"A brand-new candy-red PT Cruiser with a convertible top and a turbo-charged engine," she said demurely.

"A car! Isn't that wonderful! Ho-ho-ho!" he said, sliding the kid off his lap as soon as the male helper elf behind the tripod snapped a picture. Was he supposed to promise delivery of such extravagant requests? Tom had no idea.

For the next fifteen minutes or so, Tom listened as kids asked for Yu-Gi-Oh! cards, Bratz dolls, even a Learjet. He was wondering what on earth a Crash Team Bandicoot was when he started counting the minutes; only an hour or so, and he'd be out of there. "Ho-ho-ho!" he said again and again. "Merry Christmas!"

Out of the corners of his eyes, Tom spotted the kid in the blue velvet suit approaching. He scanned the crowd for the boy's gorgeous mother, who was temporarily distracted by a bottle of spilled syrup at one of the tables.

"Ho-ho-ho!" Tom chortled as a helper elf nudged the kid in the blue suit toward him. And when the kid hurled a heretofore concealed cup of orange juice into his lap, Tom's chortle became "Ho-ho-ho—oh, no!" The kid stood there, frowning. Tom shot him a dirty look and, using the handkerchief that he'd had the presence of mind to stuff into his pocket, swiped hastily at the orange rivulets gathering in his crotch. With great effort, he managed to bite back a four-letter word that drill sergeants liked to say when things weren't going well.

He jammed the handkerchief back into his pocket and hoisted the boy onto his knee. "Careful now," Tom said. "Mustn't get orange juice on that nice blue suit, ho-ho-ho!"

"Do you always laugh like that?" asked the kid, who seemed about five years old. He had a voice like a foghorn and a scowl that would do justice to Scrooge himself.

"Laugh like what?" Tom asked, realizing too late that he'd used his own voice, not Santa's.

"'Ho-ho-ho.' Nobody laughs like that." The boy was regarding him with wide blue eyes.

"Ho-ho-ho," Tom said, lapsing back into his Santa voice. "You're a funny guy, right?"

"No, I'm not. You aren't, either."

"Ahem," Santa said. "Maybe you should just tell me what you want for Christmas."

The kid glowered at him. "Guess," he said.

Tom was unprepared for this. "An Etch-a-Sketch?" he ventured. Those had been popular when he was a child.

"Nope."

"Yu-Gi-Oh! cards? A Crash Team Billy Goat…uh, I mean Bandicoot?"

"Nope."

Beads of sweat broke out on Tom's forehead. The helpers were unaware of his plight. They were busy lining up the other kids who wanted to talk to Santa.

"Yu-Gi-Oh! cards?"

"You already guessed that one." The boy's voice was full of scorn.

"A bike? Play-Doh?"

The kid jumped off his lap, disconcerting the elf with the camera. "I want a real daddy for Christmas," the boy said, and stared defiantly up at Tom….

*This is Mary Anne Wilson's third book in her
four-book miniseries entitled
RETURN TO SILVER CREEK,
the dramatic stories of four men who became
fast friends as youths in a small Nevada town—and the
unexpected turns each of their lives has taken.
Cain Stone's tale is no exception!*

One month earlier, Las Vegas, Nevada

"I'm not going back to Silver Creek," Cain Stone said. "I don't have the time, or the inclination to make the time. Besides, it's not home for me."

The man he was talking to, Jack Prescott, shook his head, then motioned with both hands at Cain's penthouse. It was done in black and white—black marble floors, white stone fireplace, white leather furniture. The only splash of color came from the sofa pillows, which were various shades of red. "This is home?"

The Dream Catcher Hotel and Casino on the Strip in Las Vegas was a place to be. The place Cain worked. The part of the world that he owned. But home? No. He'd never had one. "It's my place," he said honestly.

An angular man, dressed as usual in faded jeans, an old open-necked shirt and well-worn leather boots—despite the millions he was worth—Jack leaned back against the semicircular couch, positioned to face the bank of windows that looked down on the sprawling city twenty stories below. "Cain, come on. You haven't been back for years, and it's the holidays."

"Bah, humbug," Cain said with a slight smile, wishing that the feeble joke would ease the growing tension in him. A tension that had started when Jack had asked him to go back to Silver Creek. "You know that for people like us there are no holidays. They're the heavy times in the year. I look forward to Christmas the way Ebenezer Scrooge did. You get through it and make as much money as you can."

Jack didn't respond with any semblance of a smile. Instead, he muttered, "God, you're cynical."

"Realistic," Cain amended with a shrug. "What I want to know, though, is why it's so important to you that I go to Silver Creek?"

"Like I said, it's the holidays, and that means friends. Josh is there now, and Gordie, who's in his clinic twenty-four hours a day. We can get drunk, ski down Main Street, take on Killer Run again. Whatever you want."

Jack, Josh and Gordie were as close to a family as Cain had come as a child. The orphanage hadn't been anything out of Dickens, but it hadn't been family. The three friends were. The four of them had done everything together, including getting into trouble and wiping out on Killer Run. "Tempting," Cain said, a pure lie at that moment. "But no deal."

"I won't stop asking," Jack said.

Cain stood and crossed to the built-in bar by the bank of windows. He ignored the alcohol and glasses and picked up one of several packs of unopened cards, catching a glimpse of himself in the mirrors behind the bar before he turned to Jack. He was tall, about Jack's height at six foot one or so, with dark hair worn a bit long like Jack's, and brushed by gray—like Jack's. His eyes, though, were deep blue, in contrast to Jack's, which were almost black.

He was sure he could match Jack dollar for dollar if he had to. And just as Jack didn't look like the richest man in Silver Creek, Cain didn't look like a wealthy hotel/casino owner in Las Vegas. Few owners dressed in Levi's and T-shirts; even fewer went without any jewelry, including a watch. He had a closetful of expensive suits and silk shirts, but he hardly ever wore them. Still, he fit right in at the Dream Catcher Hotel and Casino. It was about the only place he'd ever felt he fit in. He didn't fit in, in Silver Creek. He never had.

He went back to Jack with the cards, broke the seal on the deck and said as he slipped the cards out of the package, "Let's settle this once and for all."

"I'm not going to play poker with you," Jack told him. "I don't stand a chance."

Cain eyed his friend as he sat down by him on the couch. "We'll keep it simple," he murmured. He took the cards out of the box, tossed the empty box on the onyx coffee table in front of them and shuffled the deck.

"What's at stake?" Jack asked.

"If you win, I'll head north to Silver Creek for a few days around the holidays…"

HARLEQUIN®

AMERICAN *Romance*®

Presenting...

CHRISTMAS, TEXAS STYLE

**A holiday gift for readers of
Harlequin American Romance**

**Novellas from three of
your favorite authors**

Four Texas Babies
TINA LEONARD

A Texan Under the Mistletoe
LEAH VALE

Merry Texmas
LINDA WARREN

*Available November 2005 wherever
Harlequin books are sold.*